THE ROOT OF ALL EVIL

GAVIN MACDONALD

This is a work of fiction. Names, characters, places and incidents are the products of the author's imagination or are used fictitiously. Any resemblances to actual persons, living or dead, events or locales are entirely coincidental.

ISBN 978 - 1 - 4477 - 0899 - 5

The love of money is the root of all evil

1Timothy, ch 6, v 10

Detective Chief Inspector Ian Forsyth Novels

Death Is My Mistress

The Crime Committee

My Frail Blood

Publish And Be Dead

Swallow Them Up

Dishing The Dirt

A Family Affair

Playing Away

Bloody And Invisible Hand

The Truth In Masquerade

I Spy, I Die

A Bow At A Venture

Passport To Perdition

The Plaintive Numbers

FOREWORD

I have chosen for this latest novel, the fifteenth in the series, a case in which Detective Chief Inspector Ian Forsyth only participated at the very end. But that participation was crucial. We had come to a dead end in the series of investigations and it needed his decisive mind to see a way through the many confusing clues to the truth.

Forsyth was the best detective I ever worked for. He is still remembered, and talked about with bated breath, at the Fettes Headquarters of the Lothian and Borders Police. Of course the tales that grizzled veterans relay about him to the new recruits have grown with time. And some of the additions make those who never knew him believe that he is not really a single person but an amalgamation of all the Edinburgh detectives who ever solved a tricky case. And there is no need for these additions. The brilliance he showed in solving the many investigations that came his way needs no enhancement.

And, of course, he really existed. I was his sergeant for more years than I care to remember. He was not the easiest of men to work with. He had his faults like everyone else, indeed more than most. But, since he was a bit of a genius and we basked in his reflected glory, no-one ever asked to be transferred from his squad.

This case occurred in the early September of 1982, a couple of months after the events chronicled in *Passport to Perdition* and was the first case involving our replacement for Sandra Cockburn. I got a lot of pleasure from revisiting the events. I hope that you will get as much pleasure from reading about them.

Alistair MacRae,

Edinburgh, 2011

CHAPTER 1

The spell of weather in the first half of that September was exceptional. It was as warm as we usually get at the height of summer. It is a period of the year when the weather is often quite good, though not usually up to the standard of that 1982 weather. It is known in the Scottish universities as 'resits weather' since it often coincides with the period when the students are swotting for the exams that they failed at the end of the academic year and have to retake if they are to still be in the university in the following session. The clement conditions seemed to have inspired the criminal fraternity in Edinburgh to excel themselves. The number of burglaries increased enormously. The reported muggings went through the roof. Even the incidence of murder grew alarmingly. So the squad were run off their feet. And Forsyth had gone off on a late holiday so that we were coping without him. Not that his presence would have helped much since most of the crimes we had to deal with were fairly routine and he regards crimes needing only hard slog and persistence as beneath his dignity. So, had he been there, he would have left most of these we were handling to the rest of us to solve. And, since he's not all that good at routine crimes anyway, a fact he would hotly deny as he thinks that he is good at everything, it is always as well when he leaves the routine stuff alone and gets out from under our feet.

I was writing a report that Friday morning on a series of burglaries that we had successfully solved when the telephone rang and I was summoned to the presence of the new Chief Super. He had taken over from the old Chief Super who had taken early retirement after the events chronicled in *The Plaintive Numbers.* Since I was sure that I hadn't done anything recently that could warrant a ticking off, and I doubted that any of my misdemeanours from earlier days had surfaced, I mounted the stairs to his office without trepidation.

The Chief Super was a tall, thin man with a narrow face which held a large nose and with a thinning thatch of brown hair, worn short, above it. He was dressed in a light suit with a regimental tie. He was known as a man who tired out his subordinates with his boundless energy I found him sitting behind his ornate desk looking a trifle harassed. He gave me a searching look before he said anything.

"I gather that Chief Inspector Forsyth is on holiday," he said at last.

"That's right, sir."

"How long is he away for?" he asked.

"A fortnight and he's been gone for less than a

week."

He sighed.

"We're really stretched to the limit," he said. "I wouldn't normally put you out on a murder case without your chief holding the reins, but I don't see that I have any choice."

He glanced at a paper in front of him.

"But I see from the records that you did once have to tackle a murder case on your own, didn't you? And, according to the records, you did very well. Kept it contained until the Chief Inspector got back from leave and solved it."

He was referring to the case that I have chronicled under the title *Bloody and Invisible Hand.* And we had done a lot better than the Chief Super was suggesting. We had almost, though not quite, got to the solution before the great man took over. Indeed we had done so well in his eyes that he had given each of us a bottle of twenty five year old Glenlivet malt whisky.

The Chief Super cleared his throat and continued.

"A couple have been found shot dead in a house in Craiglockhart. Go and try to sort out what happened. And remember that a lot of influential people live in Craiglockhart. Try not to step on anyone's toes there or cause waves."

He gave me the name of the victims, which was Melvin, and their address in Craiglockhart and dismissed me. I went back down the stairs to let the other members of the team know that we were about to tackle a murder case on our own once again and send them on ahead. And to inform them that the high command were more concerned that we should not upset anyone that that we should find the killer.

Craiglockhart is a district of Edinburgh that lies to the south south west of the city centre and is in the main inhabited by people like Premier League footballers or successful authors who have lots of money. The house to which we were directed was a two-storeyed dwelling made of local stone situated in a generous piece of land and surrounded by high stone walls. The street in which it was situated, which would normally be silent and empty, was, when I arrived there, filled with a noisy throng. Most were reporters or TV crews but murder always brings out, in addition, a horde of ghoulish spectators who appear to get enormous satisfaction from watching bodies being removed in one direction after detectives and forensic experts have entered in the other. The uniformed constables keeping the crowd in order made a path for my car and I drove through the ironwork gates and up the driveway to park in front of the house in a small space that was still available among the plethora of vehicles already there. When I walked through the open front door, I was greeted by D C Andy Beaumont who had preceded me there.

"It's a couple in their late forties, name of Melvin, who've been shot. There's no sign of a forced entry, so the killer must have been let in by one or other of the victims. I reckon that they died around eleven last night, so I wouldn't expect someone in this area to let in anybody that they didn't know at that time of night. I've sent Sid and Penny to do the rounds of the folk in the area to find out what they can of the couple and whether anything out of the ordinary was noticed last night."

"Good," I said. "Let's go and have a look at the bodies."

Andy ushered me along a recently painted corridor that contained some good quality furniture and had some expensive paintings on the walls and into a well furnished sitting room. The room had a large bow window on the wall facing the door by which we had entered. The wall to the right held a drinks cabinet and a table whose surface contained a number of framed photographs and ornaments. The wall to the left had a low bookcase running along most of its length that was filled with what were obviously novels in colourful dust jackets. On two of the walls were also central heating radiators. There were two armchairs and a sofa in the middle of the room and the two bodies lay on a lightly coloured beige carpet with a thick pile. Each of them had been shot twice in the chest and once in the face. It also looked as if the woman had been struck violently across the cheek with a hard object such as a gun barrel. The man appeared to also have been struck violently, in his case on the front of the head above the brow.

Dr Hay, the police surgeon, was kneeling beside the bodies, examining them. He was a man in his late forties, a rotund figure who peered benevolently at the world through thick pebble spectacles. He was wearing the usual shapeless clothes and had, on his head, the battered old soft hat without which he was never seen. Rumour has it that he sleeps in these garments as well. He was reputed to have no interest in life other than medicine and the only thing that was alleged to stir his heart was the thrill of expectation at the moment when he had a knife poised to slice into the latest victim on his mortuary table. I had recently, however, found out that this was not quite true, that he was an expert poker player, a fact that he kept very quiet. But he was one of the best quacks in the business and you could rely one hundred per cent on what he told you about a victim.

He straightened up from his examination of the corpses and came across towards me, drawing from his pocket his cigar case and extracting from it one of the evil-smelling cheroots that it contained and which he proceeded to light. When he had inhaled a lungful of smoke and put some noxious fumes into the room, he greeted me.

"I heard that Forsyth was on vacation," he said. "Off to the Greek islands, I gather. So the Chief Super has allowed you out in your own. I'm surprised. Not his style at all."

"He had no choice," I informed him. "The criminals are having a field day. We're swamped with work. Even the lowly peasants, such as our squad, have had to be put to man's work. Anyway, he's more worried that we'll offend some of the nobs around here than that we'll make a pig's arse of the case."

"Aye, that's the kind of man he is. Show him your true metal. Not only solve the case but tread on the toes of every bugger around these parts. They're a bunch of stuck-up sods the lot of them."

"If we're going to solve the case." I pointed out," we'll need all the help you can give us."

"I'm not sure I have all that much to offer. But you'll have noticed that they were each shot three times and in the same way. Twice in the chest and then once in the head."

"Is that significant?"

"Well, I've never come across it in Edinburgh before. But I did a stint in London a few years ago and I saw that sort of thing a couple of times. It's the way a hired killer dispatches a victim who has done something to offend one of the mobs."

"You're talking about Mafia revenge killings," I said, somewhat startled. "We've never had the Mafia around here. Big John McMillan would send any of that mob packing. He wouldn't want any competition on what he regards as his patch"

"That sort of execution started with the Mafia but I gather a lot of the gangs that we've let into Britain have adopted the same practice."

"And you think one of these new gangs has filtered up to Edinburgh?"

"It looks like it," he answered. "But it's just a suggestion. And I'd be surprised if Big John doesn't boot them off his patch before they can get their claws into anything."

"I'm sure he will. Anything else worthy of note?" I asked.

"There's that thing on the wall," he said, pointing to

the wall behind me.

I turned round. On the wall was a large letter R in red. I went over and examined it. It appeared to have been made with lipstick, the implement that had been used lying at the foot of the wall.

"Do gang killers leave that sort of identification on the wall to make sure that everyone gets the message intended?" I asked Hay.

"I haven't come across that before," he said. "But I'm sure that's likely to be the reason for it."

"R for revenge perhaps?"

"It could be."

"Any prints on the lipstick?" I asked.

"No. It was wiped or the killer wore gloves," Beaumont informed me.

"Anything else worthy of note?" I enquired of the doctor.

"I'll let Millie tell you about it herself. But we think that the wife had a go at the killer and kicked him. He retaliated by belting her across the face with his gun. Her cheek bone is fractured. When the husband tried to intervene, he was hit on the head."

"And at what time last night did all this take place?" I enquired.

"Around eleven, give or take an hour either way. I'll

be more accurate after the *post mortem* which I'll do later today if you get the body down to me."

And, since I had no more questions, he departed, leaving a trail of noxious smoke behind him.

The Millie that Hay had referred to was Millie Simpson. .She's now been for a fair time with the forensic team. She arrived young, unspoiled and fresh from her degree course in one of the older Scottish Universities but is now a veteran of the crime scenes and even goes out for a drink with the squad on occasion. She's rather on the plain side and with spectacles that don't enhance her appearance. But she's as keen as mustard and I had always found her willing and helpful on all the occasions when our paths had crossed. It was an embarrassing fact that she was willing in other ways as well. She seemed to have taken a shine to me and I had spent some time in the past treading a difficult line with her since my affections had until recently been otherwise engaged. I didn't want to snub her but, on the other hand, I didn't want her to believe that I was likely, given time, to develop a wild desire for the delights of her body.

Millie was at that time going over the room, looking for anything that would give a line to the killer. When she saw that Hay was on his way out, she came over and gave me a shy smile.

"Dr Hay will have told you," she said, "that we think that the wife kicked out at the killer when she realized what he was about to do. A nail in her shoe had come a little way out of the sole at the front and it snagged on the killer's trousers when she kicked out at him. I have therefore a tiny fibre from the killer's pants. It may or may not prove useful in court in due course, but I can tell you now that the killer was not using one of the multiples for his clothing needs. The fibre is from a much more exclusive retailer."

"Any idea which one?"

"I'm afraid not. I'm sure that such a cloth is used by a lot of them. But I will do an analysis on the fibre and compare that with the characteristics of cloths on the market and see what I come up with."

"That would be great," I said. "If you can come up with anything. I'll be eternally grateful."

"I'll hold you to that," she said with what I can only describe as a roguish smile.

"Have you come across anything else?" I asked hastily.

She produced a plastic evidence bag and showed it to me. Inside was a tie pin which consisted of a gold pin on the end of which was a large pearl.

"Since the husband wasn't wearing a tie, this must

have come from the intruder. When the wife attacked the killer," explained Millie, "she must have swung at him with a fist at the same time as she kicked him. She apparently knocked the tie pin out of his tie. I found it lying out of sight under the sofa."

"Is it a real pearl?" I enquired.

"I'm not an expert but it appears to be."

"In that case we might be able to find out where it was sold and who purchased it. Can I have it to take to a jeweller once you've done your magic tricks on it ?"

"There appears to be a partial print on the pin," she informed me. "Once I have photographed that, I'll let you have it."

"Great!" I said.

"And I can do magic tricks in other areas," she added, "as I hope you'll find out."

I grinned feebly and wandered around the room looking for any clues but, as I had expected, didn't find anything that had escaped the eagle eye of Millie.

I had sent Beaumont to have a look at all the other rooms and he now returned. Andy's a little on the short side for a policeman but he has two qualities that make him invaluable to the Force. The first is that he can pass for an average Joe anywhere. Once he's left you, you find it difficult to think of any characteristic with which to describe him. He can melt into a crowd and find out what's going on without anyone giving him a second glance. His build is average and he has an ordinary, unmemorable, innocent face, mousy brown hair and clothes indistinguishable from his neighbour's.

His second great virtue is that he could worm information from a tailor's dummy. When you talk to him, you get the impression that he's drinking in every word and that what you are saying is the most important thing in the world. He's the perfect listener and that, allied to his ready sympathy and ordinary appearance, means that neighbours, tradesmen and servants open their heart to him when any other copper would find them silent and resentful. As soon as we knew more about the dead couple, Beaumont would be let loose to pick up all the gossip about them.

"Doesn't look as if the killer went into any of the other rooms here or upstairs," he informed me. "Nothing seems to have been disturbed in any of them and nothing is obviously missing. There are one or two nice items that a burglar would get a good price for and there's a wallet in a drawer in the master bedroom with a sizeable amount of cash in it."

"So it looks as if the Doc is right," I said thoughtfully. "This isn't a burglary that went wrong. The murderer was here to do a specific job, namely to eliminate the couple with extreme malice."

"We don't get all that many gangland executions up here," Andy pointed out. "I've never come across one before. Even Big John McMillan tends to do things a bit more discreetly."

"And, if he was a hired killer," I suggested, "it won't be easy to find him. He's probably from another area, came in to Edinburgh just to do the one job and has now disappeared into the void."

"But they looked like just a normal respectable couple," said Andy. "What would they have done to get up the noses of one of the gangs?"

"Appearances can be deceptive," I said. "Since they lived in this area, they must have had lots of money. We had better try to find out where they got it from. It's not impossible that they belonged to a gang in somewhere like London and made off with some of the illegal takings. And, in that case, the gang would have made a big effort to trace them and exact revenge. You can't let people get away with that sort of thing or lots of other members might try the same."

"But wouldn't the gang have wanted to get the money back before topping them?"

"The killer might have forced them to sign a cheque

or a deed or something before shooting them. So that's going to be Fletcher's task for the day," I told him. "He'll have to find out which bank they used and whether they had a stockbroker and owned shares and the like. He can have all their assets frozen and will find out if any have already gone missing. He will also ensure that any attempt made in the future to remove anything is reported to us immediately."

It was at that point that Fletcher came into the room. Sid is a tall, lean, cadaverous individual, forty years old and with a gloomy expression and thinning, black hair. He's been the longest of all of us on Forsyth's team and will remain there till retirement. His many years in the force have convinced him that it will always be his fate to be the one left holding the short straw, and his wife leaving him, unable to stand the amount of time she was left on her own and the cold shouldering by some of the neighbours, did nothing to lessen that view. But he carries on his work with fierce determination to show that he will not let the fates get him down. And he is fiercely loyal to Forsyth who is the one rock to which he can cling in the shifting sands of life. He came over and reported.

"I've been round the nearest neighbours," he said. "No-one saw anything at all odd last night. I was told that the Melvins were recent arrivals on the scene here. They came in just over a year ago. They are not naturally in this league. He was an accountant, it appears. She was a nurse. They lived in Stirling. When they won the football pools, they discovered that the news of their good fortune had leaked out and they found life intolerable where they were. Most of the local population turned up looking for handouts. So they moved here and bought a house in a district where everyone already had a reasonable amount of money. They were known as quiet people who kept themselves very much to themselves. But they did join the local Proprietors' Association and were well liked by the other members."

"Have you ever heard of a murdered couple who weren't well liked?" asked Beaumont cynically. "Death removes all the blemishes."

"Andy, you had better do a round of the locals," I suggested. "Do your usual act and see if you can find the truth about what people really thought of the Melvins and whether they seemed frightened of anything, particularly of strangers in the area. And we'll get Penny to do a trawl of the football pool winners and see if the Melvins are on the list. Andy and I," I explained to Sid, "think this is a gang killing. So the money may have been stolen from one of the mobs, and not won on the pools. This murder would be the final act of revenge."

19

Penny Patterson arrived at this point having talked to the rest of the neighbours but having found out no more than Sid had. She was the fourth member of the squad. When her predecessor, Sandra Cockburn, had passed her sergeants' exams and gone on to higher things, the powers that be had decided that we should have a further female as the replacement. Penny came from a comfortably off middle class family in Edinburgh and was one of the most beautiful women I had ever met. She had an oval face with a small nose, shapely mouth and very bedroomy eyes. She had a beautiful head of blonde hair which fell in sweeping waves to her shoulders when left unconfined but, while on duty, she kept it in a tight coil around her head. She had a slim body with small but shapely breasts and legs that a model would have envied. She used her attractions to get what she wanted. I gathered that she had slept with the right person to help her on with her career and her development at school, at police college and while a uniformed copper. She had made it abundantly clear, without actually saying anything, that she was available if Forsyth wanted her, but the great man would never dream of using his position to take advantage of his subordinates. She had then made it clear to me that she was ready and willing, but I'm old fashioned, I guess. I only sleep with someone when I find that we have a lot in common. Having sex with someone should be the final act of a deep friendship, not done with all and sundry at every opportunity. I admit that I had been sorely tempted. It's not every day that you get the chance of taking to bed someone as beautiful as Penny. The thing that clinched it was that it would have made it difficult to keep the squad working together and one happy family if the sergeant had a special relationship with one of the members.

I have to admit that Penny is also very bright and will go far not only because of her talents but of what she is ready to make available. I don't think that she is even very conscious of what she is doing. To her sex is no big deal, using it as a useful tool in her upward progress has become a way of life to her and she sees no harm in employing her charms to help her on her way.

I made sure that she knew all about what was known of the murder. I like to keep all members of a squad fully conversant with what is happening. The lowest DC can spot as easily as a grizzled veteran something that will break open a case. I then sent the squad all off on their separate tasks, Beaumont to use his charm on the neighbours, Fletcher to look into the dead couple's' present financial position and Penny to check that the Melvins had actually come from Stirling and to find out whether their names were in the list of winners with one or other of the firms than ran football pools. Once they had left, I finished up in the house in Craiglockhart, collected the tiepin from Millie once she had preserved the latent print it contained for posterity and took it to a friendly neighbourhood jewellery store in Princes Street.

The manager of the store clearly felt that it was a good thing to keep in with the police. He personally ushered me into his office in the back of the premises and offered me an alcoholic refreshment from a small cupboard, which I declined, being on duty, though he helped himself to a small sherry while he conducted his examination of the pin. After a careful scrutiny, he gave his verdict.

"We don't carry this line ourselves," he informed me, "though a number of outlets do. It would cost in the region of £100. It would be almost impossible to determine where it came from, since there so many places sell it, including two or three in Edinburgh."

He gave me the names and addresses of the jewellers likely to sell that type of tiepin in the city. Subsequent visits to these shops led to nothing. None remembered selling that tiepin in the recent past and their records of sales of similar pins at more remote periods were to people known to them or impulse sales to visitors to the city. We did in time check up on all names given to me but none appeared to fit the description we eventually had of the killer. And that wasn't surprising if the killer was a professional from out of town when the pin could have been bought anywhere.

I returned at the end of the afternoon to the Fettes Headquarters, wrote a report and delivered it to the Chief Super. Since he had not expected us to have solved the crime in a few hours, he received the report and read it without comment. I gave a press conference where I made a brief statement and refused to give any details of how the pair had been murdered. I also declined to answer any questions and then wended my way to the watering hole that we use after work, a pub that lies roughly half way between Headquarters and the Crematorium.

CHAPTER 2

I found the rest of the squad already in the pub occupying our usual table which is far enough away from the entrance, the bar counter and other tables to ensure that our words of wisdom do not find their way into the ears of any interested listener and appear in garbled form in the next day's *Scotsman.* The men had pints of heavy in front of them. Penny was nursing a gin and tonic. I had told Penny that I expected her to be there to discuss the case with which we had been landed. The others needed no instruction. I acquired a pint of heavy from the bar counter and joined them at the table.

It may surprise you that we were about to review the case in the local pub and not in the police station. But this is where we meet to try to solve cases when investigating a murder under the direction of Forsyth. The great man always keeps his thoughts on a case to himself. This for two reasons. He is determined that no-one will ever know if he gets things wrong. So he plays his cards close to his chest and never lets us know what they are until he is absolutely sure he has got it right. And he wants to astonish everyone, particularly the poor peasants who work under him, with his brilliance. So that the solution that he expounds must come as a revelation and astound us all. So it is our wish just once to beat him to the punch and arrive at a solution of a mystery before he does. And the fact that he has promised any squad that achieves that feat a case of the finest malt whisky and the noising of their triumph abroad adds to our keenness. I suppose that, since Forsyth was not involved this time, we could have had the review in the nick. But we were accustomed to having these meetings in the pub and I have always found that a little alcohol is very good in loosening the tongue, removing the inhibitions and heightening the thought processes.

I passed my cigarettes around, Penny declining since she preferred her own Turkish ones. I took a swallow of the beer before starting proceedings.

“As long as you are on this team,“ I told Penny, “you can expect to meet here at the end of the day on any murder case. It is probably not known to you, and you will keep this to yourself if you want to remain as part of the team, that Forsyth has his own method of working, a method which one has to admit has been very successful in the past. But it is not a method which makes life easy for his subordinates. He never lets us know what he is thinking until he knows who the killer is and, what’s more, can prove it.”

“How the heck do you know what to do in that case?” she asked.

"We follow normal procedures. Occasionally, the great man will emerge from his cocoon and issue instructions. They may make little sense to us mere mortals, but we follow them to the letter and, once he is able to reveal all, we understand why they were issued by him."

"So why do you wish us all to meet here when we have a murder case on our hands?" was Penny's next question.

"Because Forsyth," Fletcher came in, "has promised any squad who beats him to the punch in any murder a case of malt whisky. If you want to stay on this squad, you will have to help us earn it."

She still looked a bit astonished.

"And you do this for every case?"

"We do."

"And how many cases of whisky have you actually earned?"

"We've never actually solved a case before him," I was forced to admit, "though on one occasion we came so close that he gave each of us a bottle of 25 year old Glenlivet. But, with your help, we might even be able to solve this one before he gets back."

I could see that the thought of solving a case before Forsyth was very appealing to her. She was, after all, a bright cookie and full of ambition.

Having put Penny in the picture, I reviewed all we knew of the case, apprising them that my pursuit of the pearl tiepin had yielded no results. Beaumont then reported that his chats with the neighbours, and particularly with the one or two of the servants who were employed by some of the residents, had led him to the conclusion that the Melvins were quiet people who kept themselves to themselves. They were generally well liked and did not attempt to disguise their more humble origins. They were not visited, as far as was known, by old friends from their Stirling days or from anywhere else, which appeared to indicate that they had severed all roots with the past, as they would if they were trying to prevent their past catching up with them. They were also said to be somewhat suspicious of strangers though this was not uncommon in a wealthy area like Craiglockhart.

Fletcher reported that he had been successful in arranging for all the assets of the Melvins to be frozen. As far as was known, there had been no attempt to remove money from accounts or dispose of bonds or shares. So, if the killer had found out how to get at the Melvins' assets before killing them, he had made so far no attempt to benefit from that knowledge.

Penny had discovered that the Melvins had not come

to Edinburgh from Stirling. They were not known in the latter town. But she had had a bit of luck. The lawyer who dealt with their affairs had still a copy of the letter when they had first got in touch with him and their address then had been in Lochgelly in Fife, though their name at that time had been Abercromby. She had rung a colleague who had been at Police College at the same time as she, and was no doubt a male who had enjoyed her favours, and was now in Glenrothes. He had been delighted to make enquiries for her and had found out that the couple were remembered in Lochgelly as a pair who didn't mix and who had few friends. Their winning of the pools was well known, though when Penny had checked up with the pools companies, none had the Melvins, or rather the Abercrombys, on the lists of winners. To be thorough, Penny had scoured the lists for a winner from the Lochgelly area at around the time that the Melvins had allegedly won, since it was not impossible that they had used a false name on their entry. But that line of enquiry had also yielded a blank.

"So it looks not unlikely," she concluded, "that the Melvins acquired their money from some more illegal source."

"Did your friend discover how the pair were employed when they lived in Lochgelly?" I asked.

"They both worked in Kirkcaldy, he as an accountant, she as a nurse."

"Then your task for tomorrow will be to visit Lochgelly and Kirkcaldy and find out whether they really worked for the firms that they claimed or if they were employed by some organisation where they would have access to a large quantity of illegally obtained money."

We sat pondering what we had learned while Sid fetched another round of drinks. Once I had sampled the new brew, I gave my conclusions.

"It looks increasingly as if the Melvins were involved, while in Fife, in illegal operations and finished up by helping themselves to some of the takings, changing their identities and holing up in Craiglockhart. The gang from whom they had removed the cash have finally caught up with them and exacted revenge for the theft. If this is so, the chances of nabbing the killer are remote. He will be a professional and will have left no clues. Our one hope is to find out what was the organisation for which they worked in Fife that was making illegal millions. If we could then break up their operation and apply pressure to them, we might get them to name who it was that they hired to exact revenge on the Melvins. And I am not at all sure that we could achieve all that even if the organisation is still in operation. Anyone have a different idea?"

There was a long silence before Beaumont came in.

"Do you think it possible that Big John McMillan got one of his goons to do the killing. A Fife gang would know that it was asking for trouble to come in to Big John's patch to get revenge. He doesn't like anyone doing things in Edinburgh that make the police sit up and take notice. So they might have approached him to do the deed for them. For enough money, Big John would be happy to accommodate them."

"But Big John's thugs don't do this lark of putting two shots in the body and then one in the head," Fletcher objected.

"That might have been part of the contract," Beaumont riposted. "In that way people in the know would realise who had ordered the killing and would take the warning."

"And Big John has just recently got in this coloured Jamaican guy, Goldie Murchison, to do his dirty work," I said thoughtfully. "And he is rumoured to get a kick out of scaring people shitless."

There was another silence broken by Penny.

"You are probably correct," she said, "that the Melvins nicked the money from a criminal gang since they didn't win the pools and there are no ways that you can make the sort of money you need to buy a house in

Craiglockhart by legal means unless you are a professional football player or a pop star. But I find it odd that, if they nicked the money from some gang in Fife, the Abercrombys didn't get a hell of a lot further away from there before setting up their new identity. There would be too much likelihood that an old acquaintance would spot them while doing a spot of shopping in Edinburgh and report it back."

"It does seem a bit odd," I said uneasily.

"And," she went on, "I would have thought that a gang that had lost a vast quantity of money would have been as interested in getting it back as in getting revenge on the people who took it. And it must have been a vast quantity of money to allow the Melvins to buy a house in Craiglockhart. Yet the hit man appears to have made no attempt to get his hands on the money before killing the pair. It wouldn't have been too difficult for the gang involved to have spirited the couple away to some lonely building where they could have tortured them until they granted the people holding them a power of attorney and then kept the pair out of sight until they had made sure that the money had been recovered. Only then would they have killed the pair and dumped the bodies in a lonely spot."

"Maybe that was the original intention," suggested

Beaumont. "But, when Mrs Melvin kicked out at the killer and Melvin possibly then had a go as well, the pro was forced to kill them there and then."

"He appears to have struck them both down, according to Hay," I pointed out. "He didn't have to shoot them immediately thereafter and wouldn't have if he wanted information from them. No. Penny has a valid point. I don't think we have the answer to the reason for the deaths quite right as yet."

There was another silence while we thought about it. It was I who came up with something.

"I suppose it's possible," I said, "that the pair were on a witness protection programme. If they testified to something that led to the leaders of one of the big gangs being given long gaol sentences, the state would have given the couple new identities and good pensions for life. In that case, the gang might have put out a contract on them. The killer, once he had located them, would have killed them but there would have been no money involved to get back."

"That sounds like a great idea," said Fletcher. "But how do we find out if they were on one of these programmes?"

"The authorities are always very secretive about the whereabouts of witnesses who have testified against a

Mister Big and then gone into one of these programmes," I pointed out. "Of course, now that the Melvins have been murdered, the authorities may be prepared to come across with some information. I'll see what I can find out tomorrow. I'll ask the Chief Super to make enquiries. The authorities are more likely to be open to someone with his seniority than to me"

There was a few moments while we all sat and drank and thought. It was Beaumont who came forward with another idea.

"I suppose," he said, "that killing the Melvins in a fashion that mimics what professionals do might all be to put us off. If someone who inherits from the Melvins wanted to get that money in a bit of a hurry, he might want to divert suspicion from the killer being an obvious candidate like himself by making it appear that it was a gangland killing."

"A good thought," I said. "We mustn't lose sight of the most obvious reason for the killing. And, if the money that the Melvins have was obtained by stealing money from a gang, making the gang appear responsible for the murder might be an obvious way to go."

"If we have to find out who inherits," was Fletcher's comment, "we'll need to find out who the Melvin's solicitor is."

"I can tell you that It's a guy called Inglis in the firm of Bartlett, Cummings and Blackthorn," said Beaumont. "There was a note to that effect in one of the drawers in the study."

When there were no further suggestions, I issued the tasks for the next day.

"Andy will go through all the papers in the Melvin residence to see if that gives us any clue as to where the money came from. Sid will find out all he can about the Abercrombys in Lochgelly while Penny does the same with their employment in Kirkcaldy. I will explore the possibility that one of the heirs is trying to get his hands on his inheritance early. At the same time I'll put out feelers to see if there is any word that the killing was done by Big John under contract. Some of the snitches may have word of that or know what the movements of his gunslingers were last night."

We tossed it around for a while longer, during the course of which I laid on a further round of drinks. When it was clear that we were getting nowhere, I informed the others that I was going home to get something to eat. Penny, following my lead, announced that she had a date and would leave also. The other two decided to stay on and ordered some food and more drinks. Both of them had been married but had been divorced by wives unable to cope with the long hours their husbands worked and the cold shouldering by the neighbours. A companionable meal with a friend in a warm pub would seem preferable to a takeaway eaten alone in front of the tele.

CHAPTER 3

I drove towards my pad in Liberton on the south west corner of the city but stopped on the way to get a meal at a little French restaurant which lies on the route. It does good business because the food is not too expensive and is excellent and it also possesses a first class cellar. I'm known there and can always get a good table and good service.

Those of you who have followed my adventures with Forsyth in the books already published will be surprised that I did not head straight for home in the expectation of finding Anna Hyslop there deeply involved in preparing such a wonderful meal that I would thereafter be unable to refuse to tell her all about the current crime. Anna was an ex – policewoman who got fed up with the sexist attitude she had to put up with from the large collection of male chauvinist pigs found in the force, left, did an accountancy degree at the University, finished with first class honours and a handful of prizes and now pulls in a hell of a lot more of the readies than she would be getting if she'd stayed in the police and a good deal more than I was earning. We hadn't got together when she was in the police. Our paths had hardly crossed. We ran into each other at a party while she was a student and she took to me, not only because of my good looks and ready wit, if you're prepared to believe I have these, but also when she found that I sympathized with what she'd had to put up with while still on the payroll. She missed the type of police work 0that had caused her to join the force in the first place and which she only had a chance to dip her toe into, and envied me my job as a Detective Sergeant, particularly as I work under a whiz kid like Forsyth. So she enjoyed being a detective at second hand through me and indeed in the past had contributed useful suggestion as to the identity of a killer. But she had been offered a job that she couldn't refuse in the USA and had departed for higher things. So I was at that time without a girl friend and with no prospect of a superb meal as a prelude to questioning on the latest murder.

I enjoyed my meal, washed down by an excellent wine and then went on to Liberton. I spent some time thinking about the murder without getting any further and went to bed early.

I suppose, since I've described all the other actors in the drama, I'd better say a few words about myself. I was born in Edinburgh and spent my early years in a tenement flat off Dundee Street. My father worked in a nearby brewery, of which Edinburgh at that time had more than its fair share, but he was killed in an accident at work when I was just eight years old. The firm did well by us according to their lights and the mores of the times. They gave the family a tiny pension and my mother a job serving food to the bosses in their canteen. As a result of that, we managed to live reasonably comfortable lives in comparison with many others from the area though money was always a bit on the tight side. And, since I had now become the orphaned son of an Edinburgh burgess, I was eligible to became a Foundationer at George Heriot's School.

George Heriot, Jinglin' Geordie as Sir Walter Scott called him in his novel, was a goldsmith in the reign of James VI of Scotland. He made a pretty good living at his craft, but an even better one from lending money to the King and the courtiers who were always in need of a ready source of cash. When the sovereign became James 1 of the newly formed Great Britain and moved to London, Heriot went with him. Since the need for ready money was even greater there for a king and nobles living well beyond their means, Geordie found himself coining in the readies hand over fist. Since he had no heirs when he died, he left his money to found a school for the orphans of the Edinburgh citizenry.

The trustees were shrewd Scots businessmen who invested the money wisely. The Trust grew and prospered. More than a century ago the school expanded and opened its doors to all the sons of Edinburgh who could afford the fees, the Foundationers no longer boarding in the school building but receiving an allowance to stay elsewhere and attend the school, like the rest, as day pupils. I was one of these, staying at home with my mother during the night but mixing with the sons of the well-to-do middle classes on an equal footing during the day. I acquired not only a sound education but an insight into a life far removed from that of my mother. She had always been a great reader and from her I had acquired a love of literature. At Heriot's I added a liking for good music and the theatre. While I did well enough in exams, I was never one of the high flyers. Although I was urged by some of the teachers to go on to university and take a degree, I knew that wasn't for me. Book learning I had had enough of. I wanted some hands-on experience. I was keen to keep on learning, but in a job.

What led me to a career in the police I'm not sure. Perhaps it was the great respect for the law that my mother dinned into me. Or perhaps it was the lawlessness that I saw, and hated, in the jungle of tenements around where I lived. Since my mother refused point blank to leave the flat in which she had spent so much of her life and near which all her friends resided, and I didn't feel that I could desert her, my early years as a copper were not pleasant. My neighbours regarded me as a traitor to my roots and it was always uncomfortable when I was involved in any operation that impinged on the criminal occupations of the area. So, when my mother died, I moved as far away from the area as possible and bought a bungalow in Liberton on the southern side of the city. I still had the odd friend in the district where I'd grown up, but we tended to meet in town on the increasingly fewer occasions on which we got together. When you're in the police and have come from a poor background, you have to make some new friends to survive.

I got a transfer to the CID in due course and never looked back. Detective work proved to be my métier I had a certain native intelligence and worked hard. I passed the sergeants' exams and got promoted. I hadn't been long a sergeant when I was informed that I was to be installed in Forsyth's squad, his previous sergeant having at last made it to the rank of Inspector, leaving a vacancy that had to be filled behind. I was initially flattered to be assigned to the team of a man with the kind of reputation that Forsyth had, since he was even then a bit of a legend, although I had heard that he could be a difficult man to work for. I soon found out that this was true and that working for him was not likely to be a bed of roses. I was already somewhat disillusioned when the first murder case in which we were involved together came along. It was a pretty traumatic experience where the way in which Forsyth conducted the investigation almost gave me heart failure and where I feared at one time that my career in the police force was about to come to an ignominious end. I have chronicled these never to be forgotten events in a story entitled *The Crime Committee.* Fortunately, the whole thing turned out all right in the end and we became an established team.

I went in very promptly on the Saturday morning intending to write a note for the Chief Super to detail our plans for the day so that, if he came looking for us, he wouldn't think that we were skiving and taking the weekend off.. I was engaged in producing this when the phone rang and the desk sergeant announced that a private detective called Alfred Carson was downstairs and wanted to see me as he claimed to have information that would be relevant to the Melvin case. The name rang a bell. I had never met Carson but had heard of him. He had given help to fellow officers in a fraud case and the word was that he was an honest fellow and one who didn't gyp his clients.

I had him sent up and in a couple of minutes there was a knock on the door and a constable ushered him in. He proved to be of medium height with a rather nondescript face, with a narrow mouth, blue eyes and small ears and with slicked down black hair. He had on an expensive sports jacket and well fitting slacks while this feet were encased in up-market shoes. I motioned him to a chair and asked what information it was that he had for me.

"It's about the Melvins being shot," he said. "I guess I know who did it."

"Then you had better tell me who he is and why you think that it was he who did it, so that I can go out and arrest him."

"I have no idea where he is at the moment," he said hurriedly.

"So how do you come to know that he killed the Melvins," I asked.

"The whole thing started for me yesterday at lunch time," he explained. "Mine is a small business. I and my secretary are the only full time employees, though I use others part time as and when I need them. So yesterday I was in my office writing a report on a case for a client that I had just completed when I heard that somebody was in the outer office. I knew Beryl had gone off for lunch so I thought that I had better go and see who had come in when the door to my office burst open and this guy comes storming in waving a gun."

He paused, seeing the scene in his mind's eye as he relived the incident.

"You do seem to lead a full and interesting life," I observed.

"It's the first time that something like that has happened to me," he said defensively. "I was completely taken aback and off balance. I was thinking what to do and how to get the gun away from him when he yelled at me, 'Where is he?'."

"And who was he looking for?" I enquired.

"Trying to keep him in good humour, I asked my visitor the same question. He replied that he was after that bastard, Alfred Carson."

"What had you done to offend him?"

"Since I'd never seen the man before in my life, I was a bit put out by his reply. As far as I knew, I had never done anything to merit his wrath."

"So what did you do?"

"I asked what Carson had done to get him so upset. He angrily brushed this aside and asked again where Carson was."

"So you perhaps suggested that he was out and wouldn't be back that day."

"I did. He let out a stream of oaths and gave a vivid description of what he was going to do to the man who had so abused his trust. It began to dawn on me from what he was saying that he had actually met the man he was talking about. So, when he paused for breath, I asked him when he had last seen Carson and this turned out to be a couple of days previously."

Carson had then asked the intruder if it was all right if he drew something from his pocket and, on receiving permission to do so, had produced his private detective's licence and showed it to his visitor. After some considerable discussion, caused by the intruder needing to be convinced that he was not being deliberately bamboozled, the private detective eventually got it across that he was Alfred Carson and that the person who had aroused the ire of his visitor had been impersonating him. It was only then that the intruder pocketed his gun, much to Carson's relief, sat down in a chair and was prepared to give out some information.

His name turned out to be Jonathan Henderson and he lived in a house in Craiglockhart, which turned out to be just across the street from the one that the Melvins had owned. He was a small man who clearly spent his life looking out for insults and making sure that the perpetrator got his just deserts He was like a little fighting cock with fiery ginger hair and a round, red face. He had made his fortune in computers and had retired to Edinburgh to enjoy his well earned leisure. The false Carson had appeared on his doorstep about a week previously, had introduced himself by showing a card that bore the legend of *The ABC Detective Agency* and announced the bearer as Alfred B Carson, the managing director. Henderson, somewhat bored since his retirement, had invited him in, given him a drink and listened to his story. This was to the effect that the Melvins across the road were retired members of an international gang but still in touch with, and giving expert advice and assistance to, those who had taken over from them. Carson was at that time allegedly employed by an international organisation that was trying to find out who the present Mister Bigs behind the gang were. Since they had received intelligence that these people were proposing to visit the Melvins in the near future, they had asked Carson to keep an eye on the couple. Would it be possible for the detective to use one of the rooms in Henderson's house as a base from which he could keep an eye on the comings and goings at the Melvins' residence? If necessary, a fee would be paid for the use of the room. A bored Henderson didn't want the money but was delighted to be part of an operation that sounded like something out of James Bond. He had readily agreed to Carson using a spare bedroom that looked out to the front. He even provided a front door key so that the pseudo detective could get in and out of the house whether Henderson was there or not.

"And you believed all that?" asked a surprised Carson.

"Why shouldn't I?" said Henderson defensively. "He was very plausible."

I also found it surprising that Henderson had been so easily taken in, though there is a well known proposition in the criminal world that business men are the easiest of all people to fool.

"And you think that the person who impersonated you is the person who killed the Melvins."

"He has to be. Don't you agree?"

"It certainly seems very likely."

He paused and I thought over his story.

"Why do you think that the killer chose you as the detective to impersonate?" I enquired of Carson. "Do you think that he's one of your enemies or a rival getting his own back?"

"I doubt that. I am the first detective agency in the Edinburgh yellow pages directory," Carson explained "That's why I added a B as the middle initial to my name so that I would be the first on the list. I think why the killer chose me was that he looked up the directory and selected the first name on the list. I doubt that he is someone whom I have known in the past who wanted to get his own back for some imagined slight."

"It seems logical," I had to admit. "So why hasn't Henderson told us about this? One of my squad must have called at his house."

"The night that the Melvins were shot, Henderson was out at a dinner which was a pretty boozy affair. He drank too much, got home late and a good deal the worse for wear and went straight to bed. When your lot roused him from his slumbers, he merely told them that he hadn't heard a thing and went back to bed. It wasn't until he got up a little later that he thought about the fact that the man that he knew as Carson hadn't put in an appearance that day and that he might have been involved in the killing. It was at that point that he looked around the house and realised that this supposed Carson had not only removed all of his stuff but had also made off with one or two of the more valuable items that Henderson owned."

"So why didn't he come and tell us all of this yesterday?"

"He's a man with fierce pride," Carson explained. "He didn't want anyone to know that he had allowed himself to be so easily conned and been so stupid as to give the freedom of his house to a thief and a killer. After brooding on the matter for a bit, he decided to take his own personal revenge on Carson and get back the items that had been stolen."

"I can see that he's a very public spirited individual," I observed. "And that was when he came storming into your office?"

"It was."

A thought struck me.

"So, if you found out about this yesterday at lunch time," I enquired, "why am I only hearing about it this morning?"

"After our discussion," Carter explained, "Henderson hired me to find the fellow who had impersonated me and conned him. I had a job that I urgently needed to finish that afternoon and I also wanted to check up on Henderson's story. It wasn't impossible that he was a nutter who had read about the killing of the Melvins and wanted some publicity by getting in on the act. It wouldn't have done my reputation as a detective any good if I'd been taken in by a nutter."

"But your investigations showed his story to be genuine," I suggested.

"Yes. He is who he says he is. And neighbours say that a person answering the description that Henderson gave me has been staying at the house for the last few days."

"So I hope you told your client to stay in this morning until I've had a chance to talk to him."

"I told him that you weren't going to be too happy that he hadn't informed you of all this immediately and that he had better be on his best behaviour with you."

"Thanks," I said. "I will certainly have a few words to say about his conduct."

When Carson had left, I felt it more important to go to see Henderson than to pay a visit to the Melvin's solicitor. But I did put out the word that I was interested in the movements of Big John's McMillan's hit men, particularly Goldie Murchison, on the night of the Melvins' shooting. I also was keen to know whether there was any word of Big John taking on a contract for anyone else. Then I headed off to Craiglockhart.

When I rang the bell at Henderson's house, he appeared at the door very quickly. When I presented my warrant card at him, he sighed, opened the door wide and invited me in.

He was just as Carson had described him. A little fighting cock who normally would stand for no nonsense from anyone and was very conscious of his dignity. But he realised that he had put himself into a position at that time where he could do no other than comply with anything I might suggest.

The sitting room into which he ushered me had been furnished with no expense spared but also, I felt, with little evidence of taste. I was offered a luxurious armchair into which I sank and a drink, which I resolutely refused. I looked across to the companion armchair in which he had seated himself.

“By rights,” I said, “I should be taking you down to police headquarters and charging you.”

He was immediately up in arms and on the defensive.

“But I wasn’t involved,” he protested. “I had no idea that the person who impersonated Carson was going to kill the Melvins.”

“I wasn’t thinking of charging you as an accessory to murder,” I told him, “though, if you had been a little less gullible, that particular murder might never have happened.”

“Gullible!” he yelled, sitting bolt upright in his chair. He seemed about to protest further but evidently thought better of it and, with a considerable effort, sat back and decide to leave it at that.

“Yes, gullible!” I rubbed it in. At that moment he wasn’t my favourite individual “Any person with even a shred of common sense would have rung up the ABC

Detective Agency to conform that the person who had approached him was the person he claimed to be before giving him the run of your house. But you no doubt regard yourself as a good judge of character and thought that checking was not necessary."

He was smouldering under these insults but kept himself in check.

"What I could charge you with," I went on, "is giving the police false information and failing to report a crime. If you had come forward yesterday, we might now have the killer in custody."

The fact that that was unlikely to be the case in no way deterred me from saying it. I wanted to get the man in such a state that he was unlikely to hold back anything, however badly it reflected on him.

"I had to think what to do," he said spiritedly.

"What any person with the slightest amount of civic responsibility would have done," I said severely, "would have been to report what had happened to the police immediately."

He merely sat and glowered at me.

"So give me a description of this man who impersonated Carson."

"He was white, either English or public school educated Scots, and well spoken. He was about your height and build. He had a round face with full ruddy cheeks and had a large nose and sticking out ears. He had a full head of black, glossy hair, worn quite long and black, bushy eyebrows. He had no distinguishing marks that I could see."

"And what sort of clothes did he wear?"

"He was with me for five days," Henderson explained. "He went off at night when it was clear that no-one was going to be visiting at the Melvins and he came back the next morning with fresh shirts, socks and tie each time. He wore a jacket and trousers that had come from one of the better outlets and his shirts were likewise of good quality. He was always well dressed, bathed and shaved and smelling nicely."

"What sort of car did he derive and did you bet its number?"

"I've no idea. He parked it somewhere near and walked here."

"Did he ever speak to the Melvins?"

"He seemed to be a keen gardener. So were they. He spotted something that they had growing in their garden which was apparently something special. I don't know what it was. I'm not into gardens myself. I employ a chap to come in a couple of times a week to keep my place in good nick. But he used this thing that was growing in the garden as an excuse to call on them. Told them he was staying with me. Claimed to be a nephew. They invited him in after they had had a good look at this special plant. They even let him have a drink, a malt whisky."

"So they would let him in again without question if he called a few days later," I said thoughtfully. "And the first time you went out for the evening, he took the opportunity to go over and shoot them. And then he vanished into thin air."

"Not without helping himself to some of my nicest things," he said bitterly.

"Which will teach you to be more on the ball in future," I said.

Seeing that he was about to explode, I thought it best to add a postscript.

"If and when we find him, we will make every effort to get back the items that he stole from you."

That seemed to mollify him slightly.

"Have you any idea who he is?" Henderson asked.

"For your ears only and not to be repeated to anyone else, particularly anyone from the media, we think that he may have been a professional hit man."

That took him by surprise.

"You're kidding," he said. "Why would a professional

hit man target a couple like the Melvins? They were the most inoffensive people that I ever met. You must be mistaken."

"We don't think so, but we are doing further work on the theory at this very moment" I told him. "And we hope that it will yield results. In fact I had better be off and get on with following this promising line. But don't tell anyone what you have just told me. And I may have to come back and talk to you again. I have arranged for two officers to call here in half an hour or so. The first will take a statement from you which he will have typed up and which you will then be asked to sign. The second will be coming in order that you can help him to make an Identikit picture of the impostor. We will circulate that and see what it brings."

I left him and moved on to the offices of Bartlett, Cummings and Blackthorn. I had only a short time to wait before the Melvin's lawyer, Inglis, was free to see me and I used the time sensibly by imbibing some of the coffee that was available for visitors on a hot plate in the plush waiting room.

Inglis proved to be a young, thin man not long out of law school who seemed happy to co-operate when I told him why I was there. He fetched copies of two wills and spread them out in front of him on his desk.

"Each of the Melvins made similar wills," he told me. "In each will the money passes, in the first instance, to the other. But, in the event that the recipient dies within a month of the first death, new provisions apply. After some major bequests to charity, the small amount of the inheritance that is left passes to a niece, a Beatrice Fowlie, who lives in Cheshire."

"Can I have the address of this niece?" I asked.

He wrote the information on a pad, tore off the top sheet and handed it over.

"Can you give me an idea of the size of the combined estate of the two Melvins?" I asked.

"Something in the region of half a million pounds," he replied.

"And, when you say that a small amount goes to Fowlie, what do you mean by small? What is small to some might seem generous to others."

"She will receive twenty five thousand pounds."

"It doesn't seem a large enough sum to constitute a motive for murder." I said musingly.

"I would not have thought so."

"And it would hardly be enough after paying the fee of a professional hit man."

Inglis looked blankly at me, but I did not attempt to enlighten him.

“And presumably the charities that benefit,” I suggested, “are respectable bodies not likely to hasten the deaths of the donors in order to get their hands on the cash.”

He looked horrified.

“They are bodies of the highest integrity. They would certainly not contemplate any such action,” he said. “You cannot seriously believe they were involved in the Melvins’ murder.”

“We have to consider all possibilities, however unlikely.“

I spent the rest of the day making enquiries about Miss Fowlie from the Cheshire police and talking to snitches about Big John McMillan’s henchmen, in the latter case getting no joy. There seemed to be no rumours that the gang boss had taken on a job for another outfit and the movements on the day of the Melvin murders of the few of his minions that he was likely to trust with a killing were all perfectly normal. Not that he couldn’t have got an outside man to do the dastardly deed.

I returned to the Fettes Headquarters late and reported to the Chief Super. He accepted that we were doing all that could be expected and dismissed me, when I wandered along to the pub. All three members of the squad were already there with almost empty glasses in front of them. So my first task was to replenish these glasses and provide one for myself. Having done so, I sampled the brew and sucked greedily on the cigarette that Andy had provided. I then got down to the business of the evening. I told them of the visit of Carson, the tale he had to tell and my subsequent visit to Henderson. I also informed them that my enquiries into the possible involvement of Big John McMillan had led nowhere. The information about the Melvins' heir, who was probably not a serious suspect in any case, was what one might have expected. The Cheshire police, who knew her well, had verified that she had been in the area when the killing had taken place. They had also been dismissive of the suggestion that she could have hired a killer to get the Melvins out of the way. She was a nurse who looked after the elderly, was a stalwart of many local good causes and seemed not too interested in money.

There was a silence while they absorbed it all. It was Penny who was first to speak.

"Do you think that we will be able," she asked, "to identify the killer from the Identikit that Henderson will produce?"

I shook my head.

"The fact that the killer allowed someone to get a good look at him, convinces me that what Henderson saw was not his normal appearance. He was probably wearing a wig and false eyelashes of a colour different from his real hair. The nose was probably shaped with wax and the cheeks plumped out with inserts in the mouth. Wax stuck behind the ears would make them stick out and seem prominent, whereas they are probably quite unnoticeable ordinarily. Even if Murchison came across him again, I'm not sure he would recognise him in his usual guise. But you have just earned the right to take the Identikit picture when it comes in and circulate it to all police forces and take it to criminal records and see if anyone there recognises it."

I invited Beaumont to give his report. It turned out that he had found nothing among the papers in the Melvin residence that shed light on where the money that had brought them to Criaglockhart had come from.

"And that's significant," he suggested. "Any normal couple would retain, if they didn't frame it and display it on the mantelpiece, the letter that announced that they were the winners of a vast fortune. But no such letter is anywhere in that house."

"Which confirms," I said, "that there never was a football pools win. Did either of the two of you," I asked of Sid and Penny, "come up with any evidence of where the Melvin fortune actually came from?"

"I'm afraid not," said Fletcher. "We've compared notes and neither of us has got a whiff of where they acquired the money. They both worked at the places where they claimed to be employed. We've talked to employers, neighbours, friends, the local police, everyone we can think of. They seem to have been perfectly ordinary people with no obvious connection with a gang. And it's a bit surprising, if they were involved with an operation that produced the sort of cash that would allow them to make off with a fortune, that no whisper of the existence of such a powerful gang would have got out even to the local coppers."

"So you don't think that that was how they got their fortunes. But how else would they come across money of that order?"

"I've no idea," said Penny. "But in close knit communities like Lochgelly or Kirkcaldy, I can't believe that a large scale criminal operation could be going on without some whiff of it being noted and noised abroad. And there is just no trace of any large scale activity of that sort taking place."

"So we are at a dead end," I said. "Has anyone any notion of how we should proceed and what we should be looking out for?"

There was a long silence while we all sat and

thought. It was I who was forced to be the first one to start the ball rolling.

“I asked the Chief Super to try to find out if the Melvins were on a witness protection programme. He came up with a blank. But it’s not impossible, and he agrees with me on this, that that lot are so obsessed with the need for secrecy that, even after the people that they were supposed to be protecting have finished up dead, they still won’t break their silence. So I guess we can’t take tomorrow off. I suggest that, while Sid and Penny continue to try to find out more about the Abercrombys in Lochgelly and Kirkcaldy, Andy and I go through newspapers and Court records of the appropriate period to see whether we can come across a case where the Abercrombys were involved as witnesses. And there can’t have been all that many cases involving the prosecution of highly placed gang members in that time.”

“You’re clutching at straws a bit, aren’t you? suggested Andy.

“I guess I am,” I agreed. “but can you think of anything better on which to spend our time?”

When he shook his head, I went on.

“We always thought that it was going to be next to impossible to get a line on a contract killer who would come in, do a job and then get out fast. Our only hope of getting on to the people who hired him is to find out why the Melvins were killed. Sid and Penny are looking at it from one angle. We will try from another. If it all comes to nothing, as I fear it will, at least we will have explored all the avenues we can think of."

CHAPTER 4

I had got in early on the Sunday morning and was sitting in the office I share with three other sergeants, putting the conclusions we had come to the previous night down on paper, in order to let the Chief Super see that we were straining every effort to solve the crime, when Bill Carter strolled in, sat down, offered me a cigarette and, after both of us had lit up, chatted on a few inconsequential matters.

Detective Sergeant Bill Carter was a fellow officer whom I'd always got on with and who had given us valuable information in a few cases, particularly in the one involving the murder of an Edinburgh wine and spirits merchant called Lamont which I chronicled under the title *Death is my Mistress*. He had grown old in the police service without ever making it to Inspector. His face was round and bore evidence of too many drinks consumed on and off duty during the long years spent as a detective. The hair surmounting it was grizzled. His body had too much stomach, again from the drinks and also from the fast food consumed in a hurry on duty or surveillance, but was otherwise in good shape.

He is a man who takes his time to get to the point so I chatted amiably, knowing he had something to say and would get round to it in due course in his own time. Finally he broached the subject which was the reason why he had come to see me.

"I gather you've been landed with the killing up at Craiglockhart," he said.

"That's right. It looks like being a real bastard. We're having trouble getting to terms with it."

"They say that it has all the marks of a gangland killing. Each had a couple of shots to the body and one in the head."

"That's it. I hadn't come across that sort of thing before. But the experts say that's what a Mafia style hit looks like."

"Aye, it is," he said. "I had one like that not too long ago."

I sat up in my chair.

"I don't remember hearing about that," I said.

"It happened just after you went off on holiday, And it had been put in storage by the time you came back. We got nowhere. Was there a letter on the wall up at the Melvins?" he asked

"A capital R, done in lipstick."

"In my case," he informed me, "it was done in red paint."

"Who was the guy who got shot?" I enquired.

"A chap called Ballantine. He had been a bus driver

in Fife who lived in Glenrothes and worked for a company in Kirkcaldy. But he'd retired early and moved to Edinburgh."

"Did you come across any reason why he would be the subject of a gang killing?"

"He retired," said Carter, "because he allegedly had won the football pools."

"Just like the Melvins," I told him. "but in their case, it wasn't true."

"Nor in Ballantine's case. But it's an easy thing to claim to explain a sudden acquisition of a large amount of money."

"Did you ever find out where the money had really come from?"

"We didn't," he admitted. "But the sudden coming into money followed by a professional looking hit made us believe he had in some way managed to do one of the gangs out of their ill gotten gains and suffered the consequence."

"We had the same thoughts," I told him. "But one would have thought that the gang would have wanted back the money that had stolen as much as they would have wanted revenge. And it wouldn't have been all that difficult to make the Melvins give up the cash before they rubbed them out. So why didn't they?"

“We ran up against the same question and we couldn’t find an answer,” Carter admitted. “I still can’t see one. You can understand why we got nowhere and shelved the case.”

“I can. But there is always the possibility,” I pointed out, “that these killings are not due to a gang wanting to take revenge. It could just be the heir of the person killed becoming impatient to get his inheritance. It doesn’t look likely in the case of the Melvins. Is it possible that the heir in the Ballantine case did the murder and then went on kill someone else who was in on the deal that got the big money in order to confuse the issue?”

“We looked at who inherited Ballantine’s money,” Carter replied. “You have to cover every possible avenue. But the money goes to a distant relative in America who seems already to be pretty well off and a pillar of the community. And he seemed genuinely surprised to have been left Ballantine’s money. So we ruled out that possibility.”

“I can see why you shelved the investigation. And it’s quite likely that we may have to do the same. But having two cases of the same type may give us an extra edge.”

“I doubt it. The case was a real bugger. But it’s your bugger now. I wish you the best of luck.”

He got up and prepared to leave.

"Thanks for coming and putting me in the picture," I said, "Next time we're both in the pub, I'll buy you a double malt whisky."

"I'll hold you to that," he said as he went through the door.

I went down and told Beaumont of the new development and together we made our way to the basement and withdrew from storage the files on the Ballantine case. Unfortunately, they told us nothing that I had not already got from Carter. We sat in my office and thought about it

"A man and a couple from Fife," I said, "move to Edinburgh after claiming they have won a packet on the football pools, a claim we know to be false. Then all three are shot in the same manner after the style of a gangland revenge killing with a large letter R on the wall, which might well stand for revenge. It can't be coincidence. The Melvins and Ballantine must have known each other, must have got their money at the same time from the same illegal source and have now paid the penalty for doing so. We have to find out what the connection between the two parties is. That should give us a lead as to where they got the money and what the illegal operation was. I think that you and I have to get copies made o f the photos of all three from the files, enough copies to give some to Sid and Penny. We'll let them know about this latest development and then the four of us will have to go to Fife and show the photographs to everyone who knew these people. Somebody must know what the connection between them was."

So we made copies of the photos, went to Fife, managed to contact the other two members of the squad and all four of us spent the day showing the photographs to everybody we could dig up who had known any of the three people. It was a tired quartet who met back at the pub that evening We were all dispirited and even more dispirited when each of us found that the others had been just as unsuccessful.

I took a long swig of beer and voiced my frustration.

"I just don't believe that we haven't come up with something," I said. "Everything points to the three of them being into some illegal activity together. But none of their friends recognises the photographs of the other lot. No-one claims to ever having seen them together. It doesn't make sense."

"If they were into something illegal," said Fletcher, "they might not want anyone to know about their connection and would only meet surreptitiously."

"How do you run something illegal and yet have

enough contact with only the odd secret meeting?" asked Beaumont. "It doesn't seem likely."

I had been giving the matter some thought and an idea had formed.

"Here's an idea." I said. "Ballantine was a driver who took parties on holidays abroad. The Melvins lived close to the firm for which Ballantine worked. It's not impossible that they used the company that employed Ballantine when they wanted to book a holiday. Could Ballantine have driven the Melvins on a holiday abroad on some occasion? And could they have either used the opportunity to smuggle in something valuable or have come across cash, drugs, diamonds, whatever, on such a holiday and hung on to them?"

"It's an idea," said Beaumont.

"I like it," said Fletcher.

Penny just looked at me with an expression that suggested that she was having second thoughts about my intellectual abilities. After a pause for further thought, I carried on with my ideas.

"As you think that it's a good avenue to explore," I went on, "first thing tomorrow we all go over to Fife and go through the books of the travel firm that Ballantine worked for to find if the Melvins under their old name of Abercromby ever went on a trip organised by Ballantine's employers and, if so, whether Ballantine did the driving. If that occurred around the time both parties came into their fortunes, we then find out who else was on that trip. At that point we split up, contact as many of them individually as we can and see if we are able to find out if the Abercrombys and the driver were as thick as thieves and going off together on their own devices or if anything of an unusual nature happened on the trip. Everyone happy with that?"

They were. After the earlier depression, this new notion had wiped away the gloom. Everyone seemed in high spirits. So we had another couple of rounds of drinks and then went off home.

I had cooked a meal at my house in Liberton, eaten it, washed down with a pleasant white wine, and had settled down in an armchair and was looking at the *Radio Times* to see if there was anything worth watching on television when the doorbell rang. I was not expecting anyone but it was quite possible that a friend had decided to call. I went to the front door and opened it to find to my surprise that it was Millie who was standing on the doorstep.

"This is an unexpected pleasure," I said courteously. "Why don't you come in."

We went through to the sitting room and I sat her

down in an armchair and offered her the choice of a selection of drinks. She settled on malt whisky and I poured generous measures into two glasses, adding water to taste. After we has sampled the brew, I asked her why I had been honoured by a visit.

"I went in to Fettes this morning to hand in a report and ran into Andy before the two of you left for Fife," she replied. "He told me of the latest development in your current case, your discovery that a similar shooting had occurred earlier. I wasn't involved in the forensics for that one but I went and had a word with Mike Ashley who was. I asked him if there was anything that had come up that wasn't in the official report of the case. After some thought, he said that there had been mention that a black man had been seen around but Inspector Brotherton had dismissed it as irrelevant."

"He should still have put it in the report."

"But that's Brotherton for you. He always knows best."

"Well. Thanks for the information," I said.

"You haven't heard the half of it yet," she told me. "I decided to do a bit of sleuthing in my own time. I've been round the houses which surround where Ballantine lived asking questions. There was definitely a black man in the area on a few occasions before the murder. And he hasn't been seen since."

"Does the description match that of Goldie Murchison, by any chance?" I asked.

"You know what it's like after a lapse of time. Memories are not all that good. And in that area, where there are not a lot of people other than whites, one black man looks very much like another."

"Interesting," I said thoughtfully. "One of our ideas was that Big John McMillan might have accepted a comission to shoot Ballantine and the Melvins and to do it just like a Mafia killing. And, if that were the case, the man likely to have done the deed would have been Goldie. And he might well have wished to case the joint earlier."

"Though I'm surprised," Millie said, "that he made his presence there so obvious."

"He likes to show that he's not afraid of anyone, particularly the police."

I told her what our thinking to that point had been and we had a discussion about the merits of our theories. I poured each of us another drink.

"I am really very grateful that you went to all that trouble for me," I told her.

"You did say that if I came up with anything you would be eternally grateful."

“And I am.”

“Just how grateful,” she said as she took off her spectacles and laid them on the table. I was pleased to notice that she looked a good deal more attractive without the glasses. And I also realised that over the time that I had known her, I had become more and more fond of her. She was not only a highly intelligent woman but had a warm personality. And we had found that we had a lot in common. I moved over to her, leaned over and kissed her. She responded passionately. We put our arms around each other and stayed with our lips together and our tongues exploring for a considerable time. I hadn’t come across someone so responsive in ages.

I straightened up feeling somewhat breathless.

“Very, very grateful indeed,” I said. “Why don’t we go through to the bedroom so that I can spell it out for you.”

CHAPTER 5

The squad met at the nick early on the Monday morning and then drove in separate cars to the travel company in Kirkcaldy, which is on the other side of the River Forth from Edinburgh. At the travel agents we found that the Melvins, while still the Abercrombys, have been twice on coach holidays where Ballantine was the driver, once five years previously and then again one year back. The first occasion was too long ago to be significant. But, on the second occasion, there had been five couples, including the Abercrombys, on the trip plus a single individual. They had toured Ireland.

We got from the company the addresses of all the people who had been on that trip a year previously. Each of the squad took one of the couples to investigate and, since the address of the people I was to interview was in Kirkcaldy, as was the address of the individual traveller, I took him as well.

"I see that the Sergeant is setting a good example by taking more than the rest of us" said Beaumont. "Or maybe he wants to impress the new Chief Super with his greater activity."

"For that remark;" I said, "you can buy the first round tonight. I'll see you all back at the nick or, if it takes some of us longer than the others, in the pub."

So we all departed on our separate missions. I drove to the address in Dalmahoy Crescent that I had been given for the couple who had been on the Ireland trip. It turned to be a semi-detached post-war bungalow in a street composed of exactly similar houses. When I rang the front door bell, a teenage girl answered the door. I flashed my warrant card at her.

"I am trying to contact a Mr and Mrs Anderson," I told her, "and this was the address given for them. Do they still live here?"

"Na," the girl replied. "My dad bought the house from them."

"So can you tell me where they live now?"

"I canna, but my ma will ken. You'd better come awa in."

I was shown into a sitting room that might have been anywhere in Scotland, cheaply furnished, without much taste and in a poor state of tidiness. When the mother was fetched from the kitchen, she arrived, drying her hands on a towel. She was indeed able to help. She informed me that the Andersons had moved to St Andrews.

"Was there any reason why they decided to move from Kirkcaldy?" I asked.

"Well, they'd come into some money, hadn't they,"

the mother replied. "Kirkcaldy is all right. We like it fine here. But, if you can afford it, St Andrews is a much better place to live. And they could afford it. And there's the golf as well."

"Have you any idea where this windfall of theirs came from?"

"It was a wealthy aunt who died and left them all her money."

"Lucky them," I said. "I wish that I had relatives that would leave me lots of money. Do you, by any chance, have the Andersons' present address? I'll still need to see them."

She supplied me with the address and I made my way to the street in Kirkcaldy, Hunter Street, where the lone holidaymaker from the Irish tour had lived. When I enquired after Mr Bullock from the man who opened the door of the semidetached stone-built house, he confessed that he had only lived in the house for a few months and knew nothing of a Bullock. But he sent me to the connecting house where the owner had dwelt for years and years.

The owner was a lively pensioner who, when I showed him my warrant card and explained for whom I was looking, invited me in, sat me down in a comfortable chair, poured me a cup of tea and offered a chocolate biscuit which I happily accepted. He was clearly a man who saw little company and seized the opportunity for a chat whenever he could.

"You won't find Archie Bullock," he informed me when we were settled. "He's dead."

"Dead," I echoed. I thought about it. "How did it happen? Was he perhaps shot?"

He chuckled.

"Shot! Archie! You do have a bit of an imagination. Who would want to shoot Old Archie? He was just an ordinary guy like me. No, he died naturally from a heart attack. He had a dicky ticker."

I tried not to sound too disappointed.

"When was this?"

"About a year ago, maybe a bit less."

"And did he die here in Kirkcaldy?"

"No way. He had the attack while he was on holiday abroad. Ireland, I think it was."

I was all agog again, but tried to be careful not to show it.

"What was it that Mr Bullock did for a living?" I enquired.

"He was a traveller. He sold whisky for one of the big firms all over Europe. And he was good at it. He was a real personality, with a fund of jokes. And he earned a damned good screw. A lot more than I ever did at any rate."

"For which firm did he work?"

"He did tell me but my memory is not what it was," he said regretfully. "It was one of the big ones and he was one of their star salesmen."

"Did you go to the funeral?" I enquired.

"It wasn't held here," he informed me. "He came from somewhere in Dumfries. The only near relatives he had were an aunt and her son who lived there. And she was a bit of a skinflint. It was going to cost a bit to have the body shipped home from Ireland, so she had him buried there. The local paper carried an item about it. That's how I knew that he had passed on. And local solicitors handled the sale of the house, so I never even got to meet the aunt and nephew. I miss Archie. It gets lonely living on your own. But he used to come in and chat. He was always good for a laugh. And he always brought one of his samples of whisky. The new people are a different lot altogether," he complained. "Keep themselves to themselves. Don't come and see me or want me going in next door."

I could see that the old man might be a bit of a nuisance if he kept dropping in when he wasn't wanted. I finished my tea, thanked him for the information he had provided and for the refreshments and headed for St Andrews.

The Andersons had bought a house in Kennedy Gardens, not at the end looking out over the Eden estuary and the mouth of the Firth of Tay, but at the more secluded end looking across to the trees that surrounded the students' residence of University Hall. When I got there, I parked close to the house, went to the front door and rang the bell. After a short interval, a woman who was clearly a maid opened the door. When I asked for Mr or Mrs Anderson, I was informed that they were out playing golf, she in a women's competition on the Old Course, he in a regular foursome on the Eden. When I asked whether they would return to the house for lunch, I was told that she would be helping to entertain the other competitors in the all female St Rule Club while he would be having a drink and a snack at the all male New Club.

When I found that Mr Anderson and his cronies had teed off at 8.30, I reckoned that they would be getting to the New Club around noon. I therefore left my car where it was, walked into the centre of the town, bought a pie at a bakers in South Street and a bottle of sparkling water at Woolworths in Market Street and consumed these on a bench on the park ground opposite The Royal and Ancient Golf Club as I sat admiring the view along the West Sands and out to sea. Then I strolled along to the New Club, arriving there at the same time as a member who allowed me in with him when I showed him my warrant card. He took me along to the members' bar and pointed out Anderson to me.

Anderson was a tall, slim, good looking man in his fifties who was seated at a table with three others, each with the remains of a pint of beer and of a bacon butty in front of him. They all seemed in good spirits after a no doubt satisfying round of golf. Anderson showed no emotion when I produced my warrant card for him and asked if we could have a quiet word in private. He took me to a sitting room, which at that time of the day was unoccupied, sat down in an armchair and invited me to do the same.

"I am investigating the murders of a coach driver and of a couple, all of whom lived in Edinburgh," I told him. "The murders were apparently done by the same person and, we think, for the same reason. And the only link between the two cases that we have so far been able to discover is that they were on the same trip to Ireland almost a year ago. You and your wife were also on that trip."

"We go on lots of trips and meet a lot of people," he said.

“The driver was called Ballantine, the couple were the Abercrombys.”

He wrinkled up his forehead as he gave it some thought.

“We were on a trip to Ireland last year,” he admitted. “I don’t remember the driver’s name but I have a vague remembrance of a couple called Abercromby. But they were a very private pair and didn’t mix all that well. In any case, why would my remembering them help you in any way?”

“Did anything unusual happen on the trip?” I enquired.

A memory struck him.

“Of course. Now it’s coming back. There was a chap there on his own who was a bit of a problem. You know the type. The life and soul of the party. A bit of a nuisance, in fact. He stuck to you like a bloody limpet and kept cracking god awful jokes. You couldn’t get rid of him. Well, we did get rid of him eventually,“ he said rather callously. “He had a heart attack towards the end of the trip. We had to leave him behind and then we heard that he had died.”

“If he was such a nuisance,” I suggested, “maybe one of you got rid of him and made it look like a heart attack.”

"That is a ridiculous suggestion."

"We think that his death, however caused, might be linked to the subsequent killings."

He raised an eyebrow.

"So your suggestion was a serious one. You think that it wasn't a heart attack that the fellow had? That he was murdered?"

I shook my head.

"The death was probably genuine enough. But the driver, the two people now dead and you and your wife all suddenly came into money after that trip. What do you think is the probability of three sets of people, meeting by chance on a trip, all coming into a fortune immediately thereafter?"

"I haven't a clue," Anderson said. "I'm not a statistician. You'd have to ask someone else a lot more mathematical than I am. But odder things happen all the time."

"Ballantine and the Abercrombys claimed that their fortunes arose from wins on the football pools. We checked. They didn't. You claim that the money you acquired came from an inheritance. Would you be good enough to supply me with the name and address of the lawyer who handled the affairs of the relative who left you the money in her will?"

He smiled at me.

"It's unfortunate that I threw out all the paperwork involved only the other day. There seemed no point in hanging on to it once it was all completed."

"And you can't remember his name or the address of his firm. Am I right?"

"Perfectly correct."

I looked across at him, shook my head sadly and gave a sigh.

"Mr Anderson," I said. "You are being very silly. We will be digging into this. We will get to the truth eventually. But it will take time and effort and we can be very nasty to people who have caused us to do a lot of work unnecessarily. Mind you, come to think of it, that may not be much of a concern to you. Because you may well be dead long before we have sorted out how you got your fortune. There is some person, or some organisation, out there in the big, bad world that, for some reason, wants to ensure that all the people who were on that coach trip will end up dead. You may well be the next victim. If you don't care about your own life, are you not concerned as to what may happen to your wife?"

He continued smiling at me.

"You have a very vivid imagination, sergeant," he said. "Nothing is going to happen to me or to my wife.

We can take care of ourselves."

"The killer in both of the cases I am investigating," I told him, "appeared to be a professional. You are an amateur. If he wants to kill you, he will. That is how he earns his living."

"Thank you for your concern," he said. "May I now go back to my friends?"

There was no point in detaining him further. I walked the short distance to the St Rule Club and gained entrance to it by flashing my warrant card. I located Mrs Anderson, who was a rather attractive, well dressed woman and introduced myself.

"You can leave now," she said, "I have nothing to say to you."

"So your husband phoned you the moment I left him," I observed.

"Naturally he let me know of your harassment," she said. "And that is my last word to you."

"Three people have already been murdered," I pointed out. "You may well be next. You know why these murders are being committed. Don't you want to save your skin?"

She seemed to go just a shade paler but remained resolute.

"If you do not leave, I will have you removed."

I left the club, returned to my car, drove back to Edinburgh and spent some time on the phone. After producing a report for the Chief Super, I wended my way to our friendly, neighbourhood pub where I found Fletcher already seated at our usual table. I fetched a pint of heavy, joined him, offered him a cigarette and we both lit up. We talked inconsequentially of this and that until we were joined by the other two. When they had also acquired drinks and were puffing on cigarettes, I got down to business. I started by telling them of the sightings of a black man near the scene before the killing of Ballantine and went on to inform them of the death in Ireland of the single individual on the coach tour, Archie Bullock. I finished up by telling them that the Andersons had acquired money after the trip just like the other two, in their case allegedly from a wealthy relative.

"And they are not prepared to co-operate," I concluded. "He insists that there was nothing untoward about the death of Kennedy and maintains that the money they acquired came from a relative. The wife wouldn't talk to me at all. They appear to be unmoved by the fact that three others who acquired sudden fortunes have been put to death."

There was a silence while they absorbed this. I gave them a little time before I invited Beaumont to tell what he had learned that day.

"I was investigating a couple called Dennison," he told us, "who had lived in Leven, where they had run a small shop. "But enquires there soon revealed that they had moved to Linlithgow, closer to their married daughter, when they acquired some money, it was thought from a legacy. It wasn't difficult to find them in Linlithgow but I learned nothing from them. They were a respectable looking couple in their late fifties who resolutely stuck to the story that it was a legacy from a distant relative that had allowed them to retire from their shop, and who insisted that it was none of my business who that relative had been."

He paused and took a swig of his beer.

"When I pointed out that three others from the coach trip that they had been on to Ireland, and who had also acquired money mysteriously thereafter, had now been murdered, I got the impression that they were a bit scared. But they refused to be more forthcoming. I guess they rated the certainty of going to prison for theft against the possibility that I was exaggerating. And I suppose it was no real contest. So I told them to get in touch if they thought better of it or if they decided that someone was stalking them. I had a word with the local police and asked them to keep an eye on the Dennison place and came back here."

He fetched another round, and I lit up a cigarette offered by Andy and asked Fletcher how he had got on. He had been to investigate the Macbeths who had lived in Methil.

"They didn't live in Methil any longer," he informed us. "He had worked in a factory there but they had won a lot of money in a competition, I was told. And who would live in Methil if he had the money to move out. So, since they liked to be by the sea, they had moved up the coast to a nice house in St Monans. I had been given their new address and found the wife at home. She was in her late forties, a small, downtrodden women if I ever saw one. When I told her who I was and why I was there, she went a bit pale but clammed up and refused to say a thing until her husband got back. I think that she was scared that, if she said anything that we would be able to use against them, her husband would give her a good thrashing as, I guess, was his wont. The man himself was out on the golf course. So I wandered around the place. It's quite a nice wee town. And I then went back to their house after having a fish supper in a pub. He proved to be on the small side, stocky and not to be intimidated. He refused to say a word to me. He said that he didn't have to and would only say anything if arrested. And then only in the presence of a solicitor."

"Did you tell them that they might well be in grave danger of being shot by a professional killer?" asked Beaumont.

"I did. He seemed none too happy about it but it didn't make him open up."

I took another swig of beer.

"And did you have any greater success today?" I enquired of Penny.

"The Ramsays had lived in Cowdenbeath at the time of the Irish trip," she said. "But they came into money in a manner the neighbours were not too clear about. Ramsay had always been a bit of a dodgy character, into anything that made money and not too worried about how kosher it all was. So, when they claimed that the money had been won on the pools, there was a general belief that this was merely a cover up for where the, no doubt, dirty money had really been acquired. The Ramsays had moved on to higher things in Edinburgh."

"So you came back here," suggested Sid.

"I did. I had their address but, when I got there, the neighbours said that they had moved on. When I pressed them for the reason, they admitted that the Ramsays had been absolute pests as neighbours. Massive all night parties, expensive alterations to the house, vintage cars bought, parked all along the street and revved up at all sorts of ungodly hours. The Ramsays also went to the Musselburgh race track and to the dog track, where they entertained and bet lavishly. They were also frequenters of the nearest casino. And, since they were punters of poor judgment, they lost heavily. Whatever the sum that they started out with, in no time at all they had worked their way through it. They had had to sell the house and get out, much to the relief of their neighbours."

"But they hadn't left a forwarding address," I hazarded.

"Absolutely right. It was thought that they had gone back to Cowdenbeath so I returned there. But I could find no sign of them. I'll get on to the lawyer who handled the sale of their Edinburgh house tomorrow. He may know where they have gone, particularly if either of the parties owes the other a lot of money."

"So everyone on that coach trip came into money after Bullock died in the course of the Ireland trip," I said thoughtfully. "And he was a traveller who sold whisky all over Europe. That would be a good cover for bringing into the country drugs or anything like diamonds that carry a high duty. If he went overseas with his own car, there would have been lots of places to conceal contraband. If he was carrying a load of stuff when he had his heart attack, the others would open up his belongings to get an address in order to be able to inform his family of what had happened. And, if they found what he was carrying, they might have agreed to hang on to it and divide it among them."

"But he was on holiday," Fletcher came in. "Would he be bringing stuff in even then?"

"His bosses might have insisted that he bring whatever it was in regardless of whether he went over on work or play."

"If it was the whole party who found what he was carrying, it wouldn't be drugs," Beaumont stated. "In the first place, I can't see a group of respectable people not handing over heroin or cocaine to the police. And, second, I doubt that any of them would have the contacts to sell the stuff."

"I would have thought that that last applied to gems or most other things as well," said Penny. "How would a bunch of ordinary people know where to get rid of a substantial quantity of any illicit material?"

That stopped us for quite a while until I had a brainwave.

"Money that's been got by illegal means has to be laundered so that it doesn't stand out like a sore thumb and lead to questions being asked by the authorities.

Maybe what Bullock did was to bring into this country the illegal takings from criminal activities some gang got up to abroad, so that someone like Big John can put it through his casino or one of the legitimate businesses that he runs and make it respectable, all done for a large cut of the proceedings. And you can't let the stuff pile up just because you want a holiday, so you fix your trip so that you can pick up the money during the tour. And buses on tour tend to get waved through at Customs."

"And that makes it more likely," said Penny eagerly, "that a bunch of respectable people would hang on to it if it was money involved. It would be hard to give up all that lovely cash and they would realise that it would all have been illegally acquired and questions were unlikely to be asked about it if it didn't turn up."

"I think we've hit the nail on the head," said Fletcher. "It all makes sense."

"I admit that it does," agreed Beaumont. "But it still doesn't explain why the people who lost the money aren't as keen on getting it back as they are on punishing those who took it."

"And it takes us no nearer putting a name to the professional killer or the people who hired him," I added with a sigh.

We lapsed into silence. I had another thought.

"Maybe the death of Bullock wasn't as straightforward as it seems," I said pensively. "Maybe one of the party found out what he was carrying and decided to get rid of him in order to help himself to what he was carrying."

"Wouldn't the Irish authorities have realised that he hadn't died a natural death and investigated?" asked Fletcher.

"You know that it is perfectly possible to kill someone so that it looks like a natural death," I replied, "unless a detailed examination is done. And Bullock, according to his next door neighbour, was known to have a dicky heart. So the locals, who wouldn't be too keen to get involved with a bunch of people from abroad, would accept that he had conked out in the normal course of events and issue a death certificate."

"But why would the killer share the proceeds of his crime with the others?" asked Beaumont.

"He may well not have intended to, but someone else stumbled across the money before he could get his hands on it. Then he would have to persuade the others not to report the cash to the authorities but to hang on to it and share it out."

"Better a half loaf than no bread at all," suggested Penny.

"Exactly."

"It's a pity that none of the others will talk," said Fletcher. "It would be interesting to know who was the principal advocate for hanging on to the money."

"But how does that make any difference to the gang not wanting their money back?" quizzed Penny.

I had another bright idea.

"It doesn't have to be the gang that's doing the killings," I suggested. "One of Bullock's relatives might have found out from an incautious remark made by one of the passengers that all was not as simple as it might be. He might be taking revenge for what had happened to a loved relative. In fact, the death might even have been as innocent as it seemed, but the relative might have got it into his mind that foul play was involved."

"But why shoot them in the way he has if he's not a hit man?" asked Fletcher.

"To give the impression that it is the gang that lost the money that's doing the killings. In that way suspicion doesn't fall on him."

"It's possible," said Penny but she didn't sound convinced.

I let them ponder it for a bit. It was while I was sitting back sipping my beer that another idea came to me. Really, I was surpassing myself. Perhaps the fascinating time with Millie the previous evening had given the brain cells a boost and was inspiring me. Because it had been a fascinating evening. The lovemaking with her had been a revelation. That quiet exterior hid a passion that I had never suspected. I was looking forward to repeating the experience at the first possible opportunity.

"There's another possibility that occurs to me," I told them. "The Ramsays are alleged to be small time crooks. They have rapidly got through their share of the money. Might they not try to get some from the other members of the Irish syndicate."

"You mean blackmail?" said Fletcher. "Give me some of your money or I tell the authorities how you acquired it."

"But wouldn't the other just tell them to get stuffed," suggested Beaumont, "since the Ramsays would go to jail like the others if the truth came out."

"Precisely," I agreed. "So you knock off a couple of your co-conspirators and then say to the others, 'This could happen to you too if you don't see sense and hand over a quarter of your money.' You couldn't go to the police for help, could you?"

I'm not sure that the others were all that enthusiastic about the idea. But they agreed that it was a possibility that had to be explored.

"What I will do tomorrow," I suggested, "is find out more about this aunt and nephew in Dumfries and see if there are any others there who might take the death of Bullock badly. Penny will continue to try to find the present whereabouts of the Ramsays. If they are skint, they might be more likely to open up about what really happened in Ireland. Andy will talk to all the people who worked for the company that employed Bullock as a traveller. He will probe about what Bullock was really like. He might get a whiff of what the illegal activity he was engaged in was. And Sid will get in touch with the Irish authorities and get as many details as to what exactly was done after Bullock died as possible. Does that seem the way to proceed or does anyone have better suggestions?"

Nobody had. We discussed things over another round supplied by me after which Penny and I left and the other two ordered food and settled in for a sociable evening.

I had not been long back to my nest when Millie arrived. She hadn't eaten so I took her out to dinner at my French restaurant, which she found very much to her taste. We then returned to the house. We spent a little time discussing the latest developments in the murder case over a glass of malt whisky without coming up with any ideas that might lead to the identity of the killer. So it was not long before we gave up and were soon back in bed enjoying another session of out-of-this-world lovemaking.

CHAPTER 6

On the Tuesday morning I called on the lively pensioner who had lived next door to Archie Bullock and found from him the name of the solicitor who had handled the sale of the house. He had been the lawyer who had also looked after Bullock's will. So I got from him not only the name and address of the aunt in Dumfries but some information about the rest of the family there.

The husband of the aunt had been dead for several years but there was a son who was around twenty two years old. He was also a traveller in wine and spirits, no doubt having obtained the post through the influence of Bullock. The latter's estate, which had surprised the lawyer by its size, though he was not prepared to name a figure to me, had been divided equally between the aunt and her son, there being no other close relatives. I thanked him and left.

I went back to the Fettes Headquarters where I rang up an old friend in the Dumfries and Galloway Constabulary, Sheila Parker, with whom I had at one time had a relationship which had ended amicably After reminiscing for a few minutes, I asked her if she could find out what she could about the young relative, George Buchanan, in particular what his relationship with Archie Bullock had been and whether he was known as a violent and revengeful man.

After a quick lunch in the canteen, I was writing up a report, to be delivered to the Chief Super, when Sheila phoned back.

“Buchanan,” she told me, ”thought that the sun shone out of Bullock’s arsehole. He was the lad’s hero and could do no wrong. It was Bullock who got him the job he has and which he apparently loves.”

“So he would be somewhat devastated by Bullock’s death in Ireland,” I suggested.

“He was. I gather that he went over to Ireland to see the place where he died and to find out exactly what had happened.”

“Did he indeed,” I said thoughtfully. “So, if he came to believe that all was not as it should be and that there was something phoney about the death, would he have been likely to take revenge on those he thought were responsible.”

“Was there something phoney about the death?” she asked.

“We don’t know, though we believe that there may have been removed from his effects some money that he had been carrying. But is Buchanan the sort to go around killing off people whom he thought had done in his blasted hero?”

“He is certainly inclined to violence when he has a few drinks inside him,” she told me. “He hasn’t done anything too serious yet but I wouldn’t guarantee that it won’t happen in the future. And he’s certainly known to harbour grudges until such time as he can get his own back.”

“So we keep him as a possible suspect in our murder case.”

“I don’t think you can rule him out.”

“Thanks for all that,” I said. “I owe you. Perhaps, when all this is over and I have the killer behind bars, I might drop down to Dumfries and pay you a visit so that I can express my thanks properly.”

“I’ll hold you to that,” he replied. “And I shall be looking forward to your arrival.”

I finished the report, took it up to the Chief Super and, after he had read it,m and at his request, expanded on the lines we were working on. He seemed to be very impressed, and possibly a shade surprised, by the conclusions that we had come to, and the leads we were pursuing, said a few congratulatory remarks and dismissed me.

Í made a few telephone calls, gave a press conference at which I mentioned the connection between the Melvin and Ballantine cases but refused to elaborate further. After answering a few questions on other matters, I brought the conference to a close and made tracks for the pub. I was the first there but it wasn't long before the others dropped in one by one. When the men all had beers and Penny a gin and tonic and we had all lit up cigarettes, I started off by telling them what I had learned about George Buchanan. When I had finished, it was Beaumont who spoke.

"He seems quite a prospect, doesn't he?" he said, "particularly if he went over to Ireland and realised that something odd went on."

"I thought that I might drive down there tomorrow and interview him," I informed them.

"it wouldn't do any harm. It might indeed do a lot of good."

I invited Penny to tell us about her day.

"I had a talk with the solicitor who sold the Ramsay house in Edinburgh," she said. "According to him, the proceeds were used to pay off debts that the Ramsays had run up. He was pretty sure that there would be little left for them to survive on after the creditors had had their money. He appeared to believe that the Ramsays were people that he thought would stop at nothing to get enough cash to resume their spendthrift lifestyle. He gave me an address but they had moved on in a night flit. I finally managed to track them down after a bit of a search. They are living in a grotty tenement here in Edinburgh. So, if they are intending to blackmail the others from the Ireland trip and have started the process, they haven't got to the punch line yet. They denied that anything untoward happened in Ireland apart from Bullock' death, which they claim was all natural and above board. They also deny having seen or been in touch with any of the others from the trip to Ireland since they got back home from it."

"Which they would," said Fletcher, "if they had already contacted the others as a preliminary to applying the screw."

"What does Ramsay look like?" I asked. "Could he fit the description of the man who impersonated the private detective?"

"He's certainly of the same height and build. And since we believe that the impostor was heavily made up, Ramsay could well be the man. He's around forty. Some women might find him attractive though he's going to seed from too much booze and sex."

Penny was asked a few more questions which added nothing of interest to our knowledge and then it was Beaumont's turn.

"Bullock was one of these people who try to be the life and soul of any party," he reported, "so that a lot of those who worked with him thought that he was a great guy. Some of the shrewder members found him a bit of a bore and believed that he was a man who had little interest in others and not much of a conscience. One of the people I talked to even suggested that he probably brought in stuff regularly from abroad and he wasn't just talking about booze and fags. But he was apparently a great salesman and one of the directors admitted that they shut their eyes to any fiddles he might be involved in because he brought in so much good business."

"But nobody knew of any connections he had with known criminals ?" I asked.

"If they did, they're not now admitting it."

"So we know that he was almost certainly bringing in contraband or dirty money that needed to be cleaned before it could be used. But we're no further forward in the task of finding out exactly what it was."

"I'm afraid not."

"Did you have any better luck?" I enquired of Fletcher.

"I can't say that I had," he replied. "I talked to a fair number of people in Ireland who were involved in sorting out the death of Bullock. I got the impression that doing nothing that would affect the tourist trade had been uppermost in a lot of minds. So I think that the death was accepted as natural in view of his known heart problems. He had some sort of paper supplied by his doctor on his person describing his problem and suggesting what should be done in an emergency. And, that being so, they did everything possible to allow the rest of the people on the tour to continue on their merry way."

"We could have the body exhumed to see whether their was foul play involved," suggested Penny.

I shook my head.

"The Irish authorities are not going to exhume without more concrete evidence that the death wasn't natural," I said. "And the Chief Super is not going to ask for an exhumation without a lot more proof than we have, if he is going to have to bear the costs involved."

"So how do we proceed?" asked Fletcher.

There was a long silence.

"I can't see anything new that we can do," I admitted. "I suppose that I should go and interview young Buchanan to see if he lets slip anything that makes us believe that he is an avenging angel. It's possible that he might even have known what Bullock was up to on the side. And I think we all have to go back to the survivors of the tour and apply pressure to see if we can get any of them to admit where the money came from. And we have to keep on at Bullock's friends and acquaintances to see whether we can trace a connection to organised crime."

And, since no-one could come up with anything better, we left it at that, had another round of drinks and went home, in my case to another session with Millie.

The next day, Wednesday, was frustrating. Buchanan was on the road and apparently not contactable. All of us made enquiries of all and sundry but got nowhere. We finished up by having a rather disconsolate drink in the pub before going home. I gathered later that Penny's contact in Fife had come over and spent the night with her as a reward for the work he had performed for her earlier in the case. She give him, in addition to what he had come for, some information as to where we were with the murders, which was just as well because he rang her the next morning just after she had got in. He informed her that the Andersons had been shot a short time earlier in the now established manner, two bullets fired into the chest and one into the head. She told me at once and I got on to the Chief Super who lost no time in contacting the Chief Constable of the Fife Constabulary. I was on tenterhooks from the moment that I left the Chief's office, but it was not long before I was summoned back there again and informed that, in view of the earlier murders, Fife Constabulary had agreed that I should liaise with an Inspector Davidson in St Andrews and that the investigation of the Anderson murders would be a joint effort by him and me. I therefore immediately left the nick, got into my car and made the journey to St Andrews in record time.

I had more difficulty in parking on this visit. The end of Kennedy Gardens that held the Anderson's house was taped off and the rest thronged with cars. I had to go into one of the side streets to find a vacant space. The uniformed cop at the gate of the Anderson's house allowed me into the garden when I showed him my warrant card. He looked at me as if I was some form of alien life but informed me that I was expected.

The house, like all the houses in the street, was built of stone and two storeys high, and it, as well as the garden, was in first class condition. It didn't take me long to find Inspector Davidson. He was giving instructions to subordinates in the garden. He was a stocky man of average height who was a few years older than I. He had a weather beaten face surmounted by fiery red hair and was dressed in a well worn suit which could have done with a press. He was smoking a cigarette from which the ash had fallen on to the front of his suit.

I was a trifle wary. He outranked me and might not be too chuffed at being told that he had to share the case with an interloper from Edinburgh. But he showed no sign of animosity and greeted me pleasantly enough.

"I'd better fill you in," he said after he had shaken my hand.

"The Andersons," he went on, "whom I gather you had interviewed, lived here with a son. The house to the west is at present unoccupied while the owners are visiting a daughter in the States. The house to the east is occupied by an elderly widow who is probably a bit lonely and so takes a keen interest in what is going on with her neighbours. It was she who alerted us that something was wrong here."

"What had she seen?" I asked.

"She doesn't sleep well and gets up early. She was up and dressed at 6.30 and was in her sitting room on the first floor when she heard a strange noise from next door. She looked out of the window and saw Mrs Anderson in pyjamas staggering towards roughly where the French windows to the sitting room are with her hand held out in front of her. It looked as if she was being dragged towards the house by a cord tied round her wrists but she couldn't be sure because the hands, followed by the figure quickly disappeared from view as she got close to the house."

"She would be able to see quite clearly," I said thoughtfully. "Sunrise is at about five o' clock at the moment and today is very clear."

"Her eyesight is not by any means perfect," Davidson told me. "But is good for a woman of her age, so I have no doubt that what she told us is what she saw. She had enough sense not to go and investigate herself but called 999."

"I assume that she kept a look out till the police arrived. Did she see anyone leave the premises?"

"She didn't see a thing. The killer may have left while she was phoning us. But it's more likely that he entered and left via the garden of the empty house next door. When the patrol car arrived, they found Anderson shot dead in his bed and the wife lying shot in the sitting room with her hands tied together on the end of a long piece of cord and with a handkerchief stuffed into her mouth, no doubt to prevent her from calling for help. She also had a large bruise on her head as if she had been hit very savagely."

"And both had been shot twice in the body and once in the head just like the two cases in Edinburgh," I suggested. "Was there, in addition, a letter scrawled on the wall?"

"A large R in red lipstick."

"That happened in the other two cases as well," I told him. "I brought copies of the reports on these cases with me so that you can see what it is that we have done so far."

I handed him the file that I had brought with me.

"Thanks," he said. "Let me show you what he did and how he got in."

He took me round to the corner of the house that lay to the south west, where we could see the back of the premises.

"As you can see," he said, "the telephone line comes in on this corner at first floor height. The killer climbed the rone pipe that you can see leads up there and cut the wires. He then went to the kitchen window, stuck brown paper to the glass to hold the shards and then smashed it. He must have cut his hand in reaching through the window to put back the burglar catch because there was the faintest trace of blood on one of the shards sticking out of the frame, though he had wiped it off. We might not even have noticed that there had been blood except for something that you'll see inside."

We went and had a look at the kitchen window but I could see nothing of the trace of blood and assumed that any other clues would have been looked for and found by the forensic team. Once I had observed the little there was to see, he ushered me into the house. He led me along a corridor and, when we entered the sitting room, I found that it was spacious with a large French window in the wall adjoining the one by which we had come in. Each of the other two walls was dominated by a piece of furniture, in one case a trophy cabinet that contained a number of cups won at golf, in the other by a well stocked drinks cabinet. In addition to a sofa and two armchairs, the room contained three upright chairs and a number of small tables, the surfaces of which were crowded with framed photographs and souvenirs of various holidays.

Though the body had been removed, the position where Mrs Anderson had lain was marked with coloured chalk on the plain, light carpet . The long length of picture cord, the end of which had been round her wrists, Davidson had left on a table for my inspection, but there seemed no clue to be gained from it. It seemed perfectly ordinary, just like stuff you could buy in any stationery store.

Also on the carpet lay an open tin that had once contained Gold Flake tobacco. It had more recently contained Elastoplast strips of various sizes most of which were now dotted around on the pile. There was also the two small transparent pieces that had once shielded the sticky portions of an Elastoplast strip that had obviously been used by the murderer.

"That's why we got the forensic bods to look again at

the kitchen window, when they found the faintest trace of blood," explained Davidson.

Anderson had been upstairs in bed when he had been killed. The bedroom had obviously been designed by the wife. The bed was a four poster with plush hangings and the wallpaper a pink colour with embossed flowers. One complete wall was covered with built in, hanging cupboard space most of it filled with the wife's clothes, only a small portion at the end containing suits, jackets and trousers. A dressing table was covered with various of the implements necessary to allow a woman to look at her best. And there were also a number of chests of drawers filled with clothes. The body was no longer there but there were two bullet holes in the sheet and blanket that had covered him in bed and one in the pillow and there was a fair amount of blood around.

There seemed no evidence that the killer had been in the en suite bathroom or in any other of the rooms on that floor.

"Where did he get the Elastoplast?" I asked.

"The son used a bedroom situated on the ground floor," I was told by Davidson. "He also used the downstairs bathroom for his morning ablutions and to store his shaving kit and toothbrush and paste. The killer found the Elastoplast there."

We returned to the ground floor and I had a look into the bathroom. The bath contained a shower stall that was still wet from its morning use. The used towels hanging over a heated towel rail also bore testimony to the son's cleanliness. There was a wash hand basin above which was a large medicine cabinet which stood open, I idly looked at the contents. The son appeared to be a bit of a hypochondriac, since there were a large variety of medicines for a plethora of complaints. There were also a razor and blades, a nail file and nail clippers, a bottle of shampoo, a toothbrush and toothpaste, two jars of different kinds of cream, an unopened box of Bandaids and a bottle of aftershave.

"Where was the son when all this was happening?" I enquired.

"Like most of the St Andrews residents," Davidson told me, "he's a keen golfer, and is in the habit of going off early three days a week for a round with three of his cronies. One of my men found out from the starter on which course he was playing, located him a fair way down the Eden, broke to him the bad news and brought him back."

"What time had they started out?" I asked.

"At six."

That surprised me.

"That seems very early. Is it light by then and is there a starter on duty at that time?"

"It is just light by then. And, no, the starter comes on later. But these four are all residents with residents' tickets and are well known to the starter. So he doesn't mind if they go off early and then check back with him when they come off at the end of the round."

"So there's no-one to verify that they actually went off at the time that they claim."

"The other three vouch that he was there with them from six o' clock."

"And can you be sure that they are not in it with him," I asked, "and providing him with an alibi."

Davidson appeared amused.

"Do you really suspect him of this as well as the other murders?" he enquired.

"Not really," I had to admit. "But it is not impossible that, after the other killings, he decided to kill off his parents and get a hold of their money by imitating the crimes that had already taken place. I like to be thorough and eliminate all possibilities."

"I guess that's the right way to be," he conceded. "But you can forget it in this case. At least two of the other three are known to me and all three are thoroughly respectable citizens who couldn't be bribed to provide a false alibi and would consider it their duty to bring a killer to justice."

"Right!" I said. "I'll take your word for it. I think I would like to talk both to the son and to the lady who lives next door."

"The son is down at the station giving a statement. So perhaps we should talk to Mrs Simmons first."

The house next door in which Mrs Simmons lived looked the same from outside but was very different inside. It had no doubt been very fashionable at one time but, after the death of her husband, Mrs Simmons had allowed it to go to seed. When we called, we were ushered in to a hall where the carpet had seen better days and where a paint job was very much needed. In the sitting room the armchairs, though resplendent with 0antimacassars, were looking scuffed and in need of a hoovering. The room had an air of shabby gentility.

Mrs Simmons was a thin woman of around seventy with straggly brown hair that held grey streaks. She was dressed in old fashioned but clean and recently ironed clothes. She offered us tea or coffee which we both refused.

"My colleague, Sergeant MacRae from Edinburgh, where there have been similar killings recently, would appreciate you going over once again what it was that you saw this morning," said Davidson.

Far from being annoyed that she would have to repeat once more the incidents that she had already gone over several times, the lady seemed happy to comply. Presumably it was some time since she had been the centre of attention and she was delighted to remain in the spotlight as long as possible.

"I'm not a great sleeper," she told me. "My joints ache a bit after I've been lying in the same position for some time. So I'm usually up early. I often sit, after I've had a cup of tea, in the sitting room on the first floor. I tend to read a book or a magazine. And from there I have a good view of the road outside and can see people walking past."

"Did you see many people this morning?" I asked.

"Not a one. There are not many people that come along this part of the road except students from University Hall. And, nowadays, the students seem to spend a lot of time drinking and socializing in the evenings. So they tend not to get up too early in the morning."

"So what was it that made you look up from your book and see Mrs Anderson?"

"I don't know exactly what the noise was. Like something falling over perhaps. So I looked up and there was Mrs Anderson in her night things."

“You’re sure it was Mrs Anderson?” I asked.

“What other woman than Mrs Anderson would be in the garden next door at that time in the morning in pyjamas?” she said rather sharply. “Of course it was Mrs Anderson.”

I felt somewhat chastened.

“And what was she doing?”

“It looked as if she was being dragged back into the house by a rope tied around her hands.”

“Was she making any sound during this time?” I enquired.

“I heard a kind of muffled sound as if her mouth was full of food and the words she wanted to say couldn’t get out.”

“Why do you think they had let her get outside to be seen?” I asked.

“I suppose, if she saw an opportunity, she might have made a run for freedom.”

“For how long did you see her?”

“She was only in view for a few seconds and then she was dragged into the house.”

“I assume that, after you had dialled 999, you went back to the window.”

“I did.”

“And did you see anything further?”

"Not a thing," she said, "until the police arrived."

I sat and thought for a few minutes while Davidson sat and watched me.

"How did you get on with the Andersons?" I asked finally.

"Pretty well," she said without hesitation. "They were a nice couple. And helpful to me in fetching things for me if I couldn't get out to the shops. Not really out of the top drawer," she added with a sigh, "but things have changed a lot since when I was young."

"Do you know how they got the money that allowed them to come and live in an expensive place like St Andrews?"

"Apparently an aunt, whose husband had been a manufacturer of linoleum in the days when that was popular and had made quite a bit of money, left them her fortune when she died."

"What had he done before they moved here?" I asked.

"He claimed to have run, with her help, an art gallery," she replied. "I suspect that it was more probably a shop that sold art supplies and some pictures on the side."

"And they have a son. What is he like?"

Her face took on a frown.

"I don't think that it was a good thing from his point of view that they came into the money from the inheritance. He has become a bit of a layabout. He gave up his job to move here with them and shows no inclination to find another one. It doesn't do a young man any good to sponge on his parents. Such easy living is not good for the moral fibre."

"Did the parents not attempt to get him to look to a future career?"

"They did," she admitted. "But they were far too soft with him. When he made no effort to follow their advice, they let him go on in a life of idleness. In my day, he would have been told pretty sharply to get off his backside and find some useful work. But thing are not what they were. Children are allowed to get away with almost anything these days."

"So he just spends his days playing golf."

"And his nights drinking and gambling," added Mrs Simmons. "Or going to unsavoury places with that girl friend of his, Samantha And she's no better than she should be. They make a fine pair. She has the same outlook on life as he has. Take everything you can and give nothing back. And I wouldn't be at all surprised if they weren't into drugs."

I thanked the lady for her help and, once I had

assured Davidson that there was nothing more that I wanted to see in the Kennedy Gardens premises, the two of us went down to the local nick in St Andrews where Michael Anderson had given a formal statement which was now being typed up ready for him to sign. We find him sitting disconsolately in an interview room nursing a cup of coffee. I was amused to see that he was sitting in his underclothes with a long coat wrapped round him. He had apparently been told that his outer clothes had to be examined by the forensic people in case they had picked up anything inadvertently from the murder scene. The real reason was that the Fife police wanted his body exposed so that they could see if any past of his hands, feet, arms or legs contained a scratch whether covered with Elastoplast or not. I was later informed that no scratch had been found.

Michael Anderson was about thirty, of average height and with a thin face that had high cheek bones. His hair was brown, worn long and with a tendency to curl which was rather attractive. His mouth had a somewhat petulant twist and his eyes were a shade too close together. The legs that stuck out from under the overcoat were well shaped and sturdy. He looked shattered by what had happened that morning.

"Sorry to keep you hanging around," said Davidson.

"My colleague, Sergeant MacRae from Edinburgh, would like a few words. After that, we'll get you to sign your statement and then you can go back home. Of course, your home is a crime scene and you will not be able to stay there for a day or two. If you can't get a bed at a friend's place, we can fix something up for you."

"No problem. I'll fix something up for myself."

"So, if you go back home, my people will let you pick up what you will need for your stay elsewhere, but an officer will have to check anything you propose to take from the house."

"I understand," said Anderson.

He turned to me.

"Did you interview my father and mother the other day?" he asked.

"I did," I replied. "Your mother refused to speak to me but your father did. I informed him that three people who had gone on a trip with them had been killed in the same manner, indeed the manner in which your parents have now been murdered. I suggested to him that the link was something that had happened on the trip. And that that something had resulted in all the members of the party coming in to money. He continued to insist that his money had come from an inheritance and that nothing untoward had happened on the trip apart from the not unexpected death of one of the party. I warned him that he and your mother might be in considerable danger. He laughed off my fears. You can see that my anxiety for their safety was perfectly justified."

"Father said that he had been interviewed by a detective from Edinburgh," said Anderson, "but that it was something in which he couldn't help the police and had nothing to do with him."

"Did he ever confide in you where the money that allowed the family to come and live in St Andrews had actually come from."

He frowned.

"He always said that the money came from an aunt that I had never met. I had no reason not to believe him. Wasn't it true?"

"We believe that there is a strong possibility that the people on the trip I mentioned may have hung on to valuables, which may have been illegally obtained, that were in the possession of the member of the party who died on the trip."

"My parents were always so upright," he said wonderingly. "I can't believe that they would get into something illegal like that."

"It is possible," I pointed out, "that the death of your parents is the latest episode in a series of acts of revenge for what was done on the trip. Have they seemed uneasy recently? Suspicious of strangers? Have odd people called at the house or been seen hanging around in the vicinity?"

"I haven't noticed anything different recently," he had to admit. "But then people tell me that I'm not all that perceptive. And I suppose that I didn't pay all that much attention to my parents."

"You went off to play golf at what time this morning?" I enquired.

"Round about 5.45. I'm in a regular four and we tee off at six. And it takes me about fifteen minutes to get down there."

"And did you see anyone in Kennedy Gardens when you were making your way to the course?"

"Not a soul. There are few people around at that time in the morning. The first person I saw was on the North Haugh near the main road."

We left him and sent someone through with his clothes.

"Anyone else you want to see or anything else you want to do?" asked Davidson.

"I can't think of anything," I replied.

"Then how would you fancy a pint? We ought to have a few words about how we proceed but a pub would be better than here."

"I couldn't agree more," I said. "Let's go and discuss everything over a pint of heavy."

We retired to the Whey Pet Tavern which lies just over the road from the West Port. We collected a couple of pints, took them to an isolated corner of the saloon bar, lit up cigarettes and took long and satisfying swigs from the tankards.

"Can I start by saying," I told him, "that I have been pleasantly surprised by my reception here. It would have been perfectly understandable if you had been a trifle miffed at an interloper from the big city muscling in on your case and acted accordingly. But you have welcomed me, given me access to everything and, in addition, not pulled rank on me. And, indeed, finally taken me out and bought me a drink. I do appreciate it."

He grinned.

"I might not have been so accommodating had my boss, Superintendent Bill Munroe, not been an old buddy of your boss, Forsyth. He used to work in Edinburgh. He asks that you tell Forsyth that he was asking after him. He told me to treat you as I would my best friend. And even I have heard of Forsyth. I'm hoping that he has passed the odd wrinkle on to you."

"I'm not sure that he has. Anyway, you'd better have

a read of the reports I brought with me."

While he glanced over the papers, I thought about all that I had learned this morning. None of it seemed to add light to what we already knew. After a while Davidson looked up from his reading.

"Right!" he said. "These are the official reports for the high-ups and to protect your back. What do you really think?"

"It looked initially like a series of revenge killings by a gang," I said carefully, "on the people who had been involved in taking illegal money he was carrying off the guy who died. But one asks, if that is the case, why are they not trying to get what must have been a substantial amount of money back as well as giving out a lesson that they are not to be trifled with?"

"Why indeed."

"It's possible that the Ramsays are knocking off their fellow conspirators to try to persuade them to divvy up some of their ill gotten gains. But it seems a bit farfetched and a rather convoluted method of doing so. So I would plump for the young lad, Buchanan, taking out one by one all the people whom he thinks killed a beloved uncle in order to steal the money he was carrying. And he is doing it like a gangland killing in order to divert suspicion from himself."

"It does seem the theory that makes the most sense," Davidson said judiciously. "You're assuming that Buchanan knew what the old man was up to?"

"I am. He may well have taken over the collection and bringing in of the cash from illegal sources in other parts of Europe now that the uncle is dead, since he's in the same business, with the same opportunities to get in and out of the country on a regular basis without too many questions being asked."

Davidson thought about it.

"It's going to be bloody difficult to pin the killings on him. He doesn't seem to have left any clues that a jury could fasten onto. What do you suppose should be our next step?"

I had given that some consideration while he had been reading the reports.

"Buchanan is supposed to be abroad," I pointed out. "We should try to find out if he entered the country yesterday, but I guess, if he did, he would have used a false passport. And gone back out again. When he does return officially to this country, we should have him in and give him a good grilling."

"And in the meantime?"

"We shouldn't dismiss the other possibilities. It would be as well to find out if the Ramsays have an alibi for this morning. And it would be worth applying pressure to them and to the other surviving members of the original conspiracy, to see if they will be a bit more forthcoming about the source of their suddenly acquired wealth. If we give them the gory details of the latest killings, they may be scared enough to give us information in return for protection."

"Which we couldn't really provide for ever and ever," he pointed out.

"But they are not to know that," I said.

"Right!" he said. "Why don't you enquire as to Buchanan's supposed present location and find out when he is due home. Then go and put the fear of God into the Ramsays while I try to do the same to the Dennisons and the MacBeths."

"That seems OK to me. Shall we rendezvous back here at four to compare notes, to have a discussion as to what extra information we may have gained and what else we do tomorrow. And, more importantly, so that I can buy you the other half."

CHAPTER 4

While Davidson waited, I called Buchanan's employers from the pub and discovered that he had arrived back from his trip abroad the previous evening, would no doubt be having a long lie in but was expected to appear at the headquarters in Dumfries later in the day. I got from them Buchanan's telephone number, called the man and told him to stay at home till I got there since I was driving down immediately.

My trip to the south west meant that we would have to change our plans for the day. Davidson would have to take on the task of screwing the Ramsays into the ground as well as putting the fear of God into the Dennisons and the MacBeths.

It took me two hours and a half to get to the house where Buchanan stayed, which stood on a patch of ground among trees in an isolated position north of Dumfries. I realised that it would have been easy for Buchanan to have slipped out of the house, driven to St Andrews, killed the Andersons, driven back and got back into the house without anyone being the wiser.

Buchanan proved to be a small, stocky fellow, very much on the brash side. He had a round, mean face which wore a perpetual grin, with small eyes and a bulbous nose. His brown hair was kept short and smoothed down over his pumpkin shaped head. He was dressed casually in expensive slacks, a polonecked sweater and loafers. I had a good look at his hands and wrists but nowhere was there any sign of an Elastoplast or of a cut.

"I can't think why a policeman from Edinburgh should wish to see me," he said as he ushered me into the house. "I lead a blameless life."

I made no comment and he ushered me into a chair in his sitting room, offered me an alcoholic drink, which I refused, and a coffee, which I accepted. While he went off to the kitchen to make the coffee, I studied the room. It was expensively furnished but showed little sign of either taste or character.

When he returned, I took a sip of the coffee he had provided and then started the proceedings.

"Your uncle, like you, was a representative who sold whisky and other drinks to companies all around Europe. He died while he was enjoying a holiday in Ireland. All the people who were on that trip with him suddenly became quite wealthy. A remarkable coincidence, wouldn't you agree?"

He shrugged and waited for me to continue.

"The next remarkable coincidence," I went on, "is that these people are now being murdered one after the other. Have you any comment on that?"

"It does seem very odd," he said after a short silence. "But there's no doubt a suitable explanation."

"I'm sure there is. Let me put to you a theory that we have come up with. Your uncle, we believe, collected mob money as he went around Europe doing his normal job. He brought it back to the UK where it was laundered so that it could be used without fear of arousing unwanted attention. His job meant that he could move around without suspicion and he would be well paid for doing this job on the side. Looking at his finances, he appeared to spend a good deal more than he earned from his job with the firm."

"He was a betting man and good at it," Buchanan came in quickly.

"Nobody's that good," I said. "And where did the money that the others suddenly acquired come from if not from what Bullock was carrying?"

I stopped and looked at him searchingly. He shrugged again.

"It's your theory," he said.

"The killings, we thought, might be the mob taking revenge for the stealing of their money. But we couldn't explain why they wouldn't attempt to recover the money from the victims before polishing them off."

I paused and he came in, still with that supercilious smile on his face.

"And did you find an explanation for that as well?" he asked.

"We came up with a not unlikely possibility," I admitted. "We understand that you were on great terms with your uncle. You thought him the greatest thing to appear on the scene since sliced bread, we hear. If you had come to the conclusion that the others on the trip had helped him along to the grave, or maybe just stood around while he had his heart attack and made no effort to help him, in order to get their hands on the money that he was carrying, I guess you'd have wanted to show them that they couldn't do that to someone as special to you as he was. And you would just have wanted them dead. You wouldn't have been concerned about the money they had acquired. It wasn't yours, after all."

His smile appeared to me to have become a trifle strained.

"You're accusing me of going around knocking off people to revenge my uncle. Is that it? You're mad. My uncle's death was an accident. No-one killed him. So why would I want revenge? And all this rubbish about money laundering. It's just ludicrous."

"Is it?" I asked. "It's even been suggested that you

might have taken over that particular job from him. One word from me and you will find all your stuff being gone through with a fine toothcomb at every frontier that you cross. Your bosses are not going to be too chuffed if their money is confiscated. And you will be no use to them if you are always searched whenever you come to a customs barrier."

He had paled a mite and his smile seemed somewhat fixed.

"Where were you at around 6.30 this morning?" I went on.

"Where the bloody hell do you think? I was in my bed fast asleep?"

"Can any lucky lady, or indeed gentleman, confirm that?" I enquired.

"Are you accusing me of being a poof?" he said furiously.

"Just answer the question."

"I was on my own."

"So no-one can testify that you weren't in St Andrews murdering a couple there."

"I don't have to prove anything. I didn't leave here at any time during the night and it's up to you to prove otherwise."

"I got the number of your car from the DVLC before I

came here," I informed him. "People will be looking at all the cameras between here and St Andrews to see if they can spot your car anywhere en route. I'm sure that I will be back to see you again. Don't go anywhere where we can't get in touch with you."

And on that note I left him. There was no doubt that he was a very worried man. Whether this was because he was the killer and was shocked that we were on to him or whether the suggestion I had made about his taking over his uncle's cash collection business had struck home was not clear. I was pretty certain that my talk on the latter subject had hit a chord. And he would now be wondering what he should tell his criminal masters since he would be convinced that he would be subject to intense scrutiny the next time he crossed a frontier. And not without cause. It would be both my duty and my pleasure to pass on my thoughts about Buchanan's likely job on the side to Customs and Excise.

I made good time back to St Andrews, parked in South Street and went into the Whey Pet Tavern. It was a good deal more crowded than it had been that morning but Davidson had managed to capture a corner table and was sitting there, drinking a beer and looking thoughtful. I picked up a pint of heavy, went across and joined him and offered him a cigarette. He accepted and we both lit up.

He took a long drag and swallowed a good quantity of beer before he asked how I had got on. I gave him a detailed account of my visit to Buchanan, at the end of which he sat and absorbed it.

"Do you thing that he's the guilty man we're looking for?" he asked.

"He's definitely a guilty man," I replied. "But of what I'm not sure. He has almost certainly taken over his uncle's job of bringing in whatever it was for the mob. Whether he is the killer of all the people who were on the fatal trip is more questionable. But he's the only one on our books who looks a good prospect. Unless you came up with something on the Ramsays."

"I'm afraid not," he said. "I applied a lot of pressure but got nowhere. They've sailed close enough to the law on enough occasions in the past to know to keep shtumm. But they have no alibi for last night apart from their story of being in bed together and rising very late. And that's not worth a damn. I'm sure from the way that they acted that they were up to no good doing something this morning. And Ramsay has a fresh cut on one hand. But so do lots of people. We can't link them to the Anderson murders unless we get a bit more on them."

"Disappointing," I said. "Any more luck with the Dennisons or MacBeths?"

"All four of them are dead scared, particularly Mrs Dennison," he reported. "If we could prise her away from her husband and grill her, I'm sure that she would break down and tell us what really happened in Ireland. But he is guarding her like a hawk. And, of course, they all face a sure, and highly unpleasant, time in gaol if they admit anything, and they can hope that we catch the killer before he gets round to them. And I suppose that they might even prefer death to going to gaol and coming out to a poverty stricken future."

"Having tasted the good life," I agreed, "it might be too difficult to give it up."

"As a matter of interest, Dennison has an Elastoplast on his wrist. But it may mean nothing."

"If he's the killer, he would be pretty stupid to leave an Elastoplast in plain view when he knew we would see lots of the stuff scattered around in the living room in St Andrews."

"On the other hand, it could be a double bluff," Davidson suggested. "We would know he wouldn't be that stupid if he was the killer and therefore we would eliminate him from our list of suspects."

"That would be taking a big chance. We might just think him stupid and guilty."

"You may be right. So where do you think that we

should go from here?"

"I'm damned if I know," I was forced to admit. "If the survey of the cameras shows Buchanan out and about and heading in this direction, we can have him in and grill him. But he may well know where the cameras are located and have used a route that avoids them. Or he may well have used false plates if he was on a mission to kill. And, if we have no evidence that he was out and about, all we have left is to keep on at the people we know about and hope that one of them will crack."

I took another swig of beer.

"But I've been on this case a few days now and have been working flat out. I don't see anything urgent that needs doing, and I need a break. So I propose to have a day off tomorrow unless something hot arrives on the scene."

"I'm not sure that the lines you propose will lead to anything," he said gloomily. "All right. You have your day off. I'll have another go at the three couples I saw today. But I don't expect something to come of it."

We sat like that for a little time mulling over the options in our minds. It was Davidson who broke the silence.

"Your boss is on holiday they say. When does he get back?"

"I assume that it's Sunday. He's due back in the nick on Monday."

"He's supposed to be a bit of a whiz kid, isn't he?" he said thoughtfully. "Maybe he will see something that we are missing."

"He's been pretty good in the past," I had to admit. "But I don't see that he could come up with anything we haven't thought of."

I suppose that a cock should immediately have crowed thrice or that there should at least have been some sign that I was denying the genius of my boss. But, in truth, the world went on as normal.

"He will no doubt put an appearance on Monday," I said. "I will show him what we've got and he can have a go at a solution then. Maybe he will see a way forward. We can only hope. But, whatever happens, I'll keep you posted."

I bought a round which we consumed in a gloomy silence and then I set off for Edinburgh. No interesting new thoughts came to me on the drive back. I stopped before I got home at the French restaurant I mentioned earlier and ate well. When I got to my house in Liberton, there were a couple of messages on the answer phone. The first was from Beaumont detailing the little that the squad had learned that day, nothing in the report taking us any further forward.

The second call I was surprised to find was from Forsyth. He suggested that I give him a call when I returned from wherever I had been.

I rang his number and heard the familiar voice announcing his name. When I had told him who was on the other end of the phone, he thanked me for returning his call.

"I returned from Greece today," he continued. "intending to have a quiet weekend at home before returning to work. But I am led to believe that you are in the middle of a tricky case. Far be it from me to interfere in a case that you are conducting," he said, lying in his teeth, since he wouldn't let a consideration like that stand in his way if he wanted to get involved in a case that held a stimulating intellectual challenge, "but I thought I would ascertain how you were progressing and, if you felt the need for it, perhaps offer you some advice."

"I could do with some advice," I confessed. "We are at a bit of a dead end."

"Would you care to come round to my place and fill me in over a glass of whisky?" he asked. "If it's not too much of a bother."

"I'd be delighted," I admitted.

So fifteen minutes later I was sitting in the great

man's sitting room where he was pouring out for each of us a substantial glass of Glenlivet malt whisky to which we added a soupcon of Highland spring water to taste. I told him all that had happened, and all the theories that we had come up with, after which he refilled the glasses and sat in thought for some time. As he did so, I sat and studied him as I had done so often in the past.

I suppose that it might be appropriate for me to give you a bit about Forsyth and his background. He is an imposing figure, an adjective that can also be applied to the way in which he deals with the hired help. He is 6' 4" with a large-boned, quite athletic frame which he keeps in reasonable nick with exercise and golf. A shock of blonde hair stands up above the broad forehead that crowns his long, rather distinguished face and a luxuriant moustache adorns, to be kind about it, his upper lip.

Forsyth's origins are somewhat obscure though I gather that he was born somewhere in the Highlands to a reasonably well-off family, but that he was educated at an exclusive public school in Edinburgh and then at the University there. What qualification he finished up with, I don't know, but I would expect it to have been a first class honours degree in something like the old-style Mathematics and Natural Philosophy Arts course. That would be consistent with both his logical mind and the fact that he is interested in, and very well read in, the Arts. He was married at quite an early age but the union didn't turn out too well and ended in a very acrimonious divorce. This may explain his secretiveness and his unwillingness to leave himself open to criticism or to be shown to be in the wrong in any matter. He now lives alone, very well looked after by a housekeeper who is not only competent but an excellent cook. He enjoys a social life that includes golf at one of the more exclusive courses, bridge at one of the local clubs in Edinburgh, concerts and the theatre and allows him to mix with the great and the good in the higher echelons of Edinburgh society. We don't see all that much of him outside working hours though we are invited round to his house in a fairly exclusive area of Edinburgh for dinner from time to time and are always well looked after, superbly fed and supplied with a sufficiency of excellent wine and spirits.

It is not clear why Forsyth chose the police force as a career. He would have succeeded at almost job he had decided to pursue. It is also difficult to imagine how he endured the years as a humble footslogger without resigning in frustration or being thrown out on his ear by outraged superiors, or how he ever achieved promotion to his present elevated rank. It is probable that in these days he had not yet acquired his later arrogance and was more prepared to conform and to turn that massive intellect to trivial and uninspiring tasks. Legend has it that one of his more perceptive superiors recognised his qualities and took the trouble to steer him gently through the troubled waters to his present safe and well-fitting niche. Stories abound of the sudden flashes of genius from him that illuminated the impenetrable dark of difficult cases, endearing him to the high and mighty and leading to his elevation but I doubt that his rise from the ranks happened that way and I strongly suspect that most of the examples quoted are apocryphal.

It says much for the Lothian and Borders Police that they are prepared to put up with a Chief Inspector who is bored by ninety per cent of his job and, in consequence, is worse than useless at it, in order to have him available when the other ten per cent appears on the scene. I suppose that it also says much for the squads whom he has commanded that they are also prepared to put up with him. Not that those at the bottom of the pile in any police force have much say in their fate. Though those of us who work under him often resent being landed with jobs he should be doing as well as our own, and spend a good deal of our time taking the mickey when he's at his most infuriating or arrogant, we would defend him to the death against any outsider. He has pulled too many chestnuts out of the fire for us in the past and, despite the appalling conceit of the man in assuming that we will be delighted to do, without a murmur of dissent, all the hard graft he should be tackling himself, we know that he has fought for us when we have got into trouble and always makes sure that we share in the credit when he has cracked one of the big ones. We have a real love-hate relation with him but no-one has ever asked to be shifted from his squad.

It was some time before Forsyth stirred himself. He looked across at me.

"Would you object if I caused a few enquiries to be put in train?" he asked.

"By no means," I said. "I would be delighted if you can help towards a solution."

I looked at him with dawning suspicion.

"Does this mean that you had some idea who the killer is?"

He tried, without much success, to look modest.

"There seems to me," he said carefully, "to be a strong indication as to the identity of the person or persons responsible for the murders."

"So, who is it?"

It was ridiculous of me to have expected him to give a straight answer to such a direct question. He will never give an indication of his thinking until he is absolutely sure that he has got it right. This for two reasons. In the first place, he thinks it would be damaging for his reputation if it were ever known that he had got it wrong. And, secondly, once he has the case all sewn up, it is imperative that the astonished natives are overwhelmed by his brilliant analysis. So no inkling of what he is thinking must ever be given until the final denouement.

"I would like to check a few items to see whether my ideas are correct," he said, "before I say anything. I would not like to influence your thinking with some unverified imaginings."

I have to admit that he is excellent at denying you information without giving offence. I sighed.

"Right!" I said, draining my glass and then getting to my feet. "Thank you for the drink. I will leave you to get on with your enquiries and will hope to see you, bright eyed and bushy tailed, on Monday morning coming into Headquarters with the killer hogtied and slung effortlessly across your shoulders."

I spent Saturday briefly in the nick producing a report and the rest of that day and Sunday in the company of Millie in a variety of pursuits, a large amount of these taking place in bed, and gave no thought to the case. After all, Forsyth was now in the game and I could leave it all to him. On Monday morning I arrived at the Fettes

Headquarters to find Forsyth already there. This was so unusual that I was convinced that the case was already solved or in process of being so. When I bearded him in his office, the beaming smile that he gave me told me that my supposition was indeed correct.

"My dear Alistair," he greeted me. He is always at his most effusive when he has just solved a case. "You will be delighted to know that the person, or persons. responsible for the killings now lie behind bars in St Andrews. But you will forgive me if I rush off. I have one or two chores still to attend to and then I have to brief the Chief Constable and the Chief Super on the solution to the case, so that they will not appear too ignorant if quizzed on it by the press. It will be interesting to see if our new Chief Super is any better than his predecessor in absorbing and understanding logical arguments.

"But I shall, as usual at the completion of a case, be buying drinks for the squad in our local hostelry," he added. "Will you be good enough to let the others know of the arrangement? Shall we meet at 12.30?"

And, with that, he bustled past me and was gone. I was, as usual, the subject of a number of conflicting emotions. I was filled with usual gladness that another case had been brought to a successful conclusion. But I was also sad that we had once again failed to beat the great man to the punch. And I was as usual annoyed that he had given no hint that would have allowed me to work out his solution. But there was no point in worrying about it. That was the way that Forsyth was. I went off to find the rest of the squad to let them have the glad news.

All the facts necessary to arrive by logical deduction, as Forsyth has done, at the name of the person, or persons, who killed Ballantine, the Melvins and the Andersons have been given. If you decide to try to get to that solution before you read the final chapter, good luck to you.

Alistair MacRae

CHAPTER 5

At 12.30 the squad was seated at our usual table in the pub, pints of heavy in front of the males, a gin and tonic before Penny and a large Glenlivet malt whisky in front of the place that Forsyth would eventually occupy. Forsyth buying us a drink is not quite what it seems. It is true that he will eventually buy a round, two if the session is a prolonged one. But he always arrives late and he expects a glass of his favourite malt to be awaiting him.

A few moments after the allotted hour, the great man put in an appearance. He stepped blithely through the door and stood looking around to see where we were sitting. Since he is perfectly well aware that we always occupy the same table and he knows which one that is, the pause in the doorway is to give time to the other denizens of the hostelry to see what distinguished person has arrived. Since the patrons have short memories and his latest triumph had not yet reached the ears of the television studios, his arrival went unnoticed. Unperturbed, he walked over to our table, greeted us effusively, sat down and took a long swallow of the contents of his glass. Only after these preliminaries was he prepared to tell us his solution.

"The case that you have been attempting to solve in my absence," he began, "was one in which you made a large number of correct deductions but did not eventually put them all together in the correct order which would have allowed you to arrive at the solution."

He paused and took another swallow of the amber liquid in his glass.

"You originally believed," he went on, "that the first killing you investigated was done by a gangland hit man because the fortune the couple had acquired had been stolen from one of the mobs. But you had second thoughts when there appeared to be no attempt to recover the stolen money as there surely would have been if a mob taking revenge was involved."

He took another swallow of the malt whisky.

"You suggested that the method of killing," he went on, "might have been a deliberate attempt to sidetrack you, but could find no other reason why the Melvins should have been killed since there was not an heir who inherited a substantial amount of their money. And you lost sight of this in the subsequent investigation."

"It didn't seem relevant," objected Penny.

Forsyth ignored the interruption.

"The information you received from Sergeant Carter," he went on, "appeared to establish that the reason for the killings lay at the point in the past when the paths of the murdered people had intersected. And your final theory that, after Bullock had died, the other travellers had come across money to be laundered that the rep had been carrying and hung on to it, is certainly correct. The person in custody has confirmed it."

"So who is the person in custody?" asked Penny.

The Chief was not to be prevented from telling his story in the way that would most impress.

"All in good time," he said. "In the murder of Bullock, the method of killing and the R on the wall were intended to put the police off the scent. And, in the Melvin killing, we see the killer again leaving clues that were intended to confuse and this time increasing their number. He allowed himself to be seen but almost certainly the Identikit picture that was produced bore little resemblance to what the murderer really looked like. And the tiepin had been deliberately left at the scene because it could not be traced back to the killer. What hit man would wear, when going for a killing, something that could be knocked off and help to identify him? The tiepin had been stolen somewhere or bought at a car boot sale and the latent print on it was not his."

"So you think that the killer was attempting at every murder to confuse us?" asked Fletcher.

"I do. And I believe," he added, rather unkindly, "that, in the final murder, he managed to achieve what he had hoped to do."

There was a silence while he waited to see how we would react to the statement.

"So where did we go wrong?" I finally asked.

"That murder contained a number of differences from the previous ones," he explained. "In he first place, the murderer broke into the house, which he had never done before. And he did not kill the lady of the house immediately after he had killed her husband but, for some reason, took her downstairs, tied her hands together and stuffed a handkerchief into her mouth. Even worse, he allowed her to get out of the house where she was seen by a neighbour. I am surprised that you did not find that all these events constituted extraordinary behaviour. In addition, had he not left the Elastoplasts lying around in the living room, the forensic team might have missed the fact that there was the merest trace of blood on a sliver of glass in the window frame."

"So you think that all these things were there to put us off?" enquired Beaumont.

"I do."

He was too polite to suggest that we had been incredibly gullible to believe otherwise but he obviously thought it.

"Why did he not get into the house by calling there

as he had before?" he asked.

"The previous murders would have made the Andersons suspicious of strangers," I suggested. "This might be the only way that he could get easily into the house."

"It was certainly meant to say to us," he agreed, "that he had no easier way to get in to the house. And the fact that Mrs Anderson was seen still alive at 6.30 was intended to fix in our minds that she and her husband had been killed after that time."

"Well. Hadn't they?" asked Fletcher.

Forsyth ignored the question.

"And the Elastoplasts scattered over the floor were meant to convince us that the killer would have on his hand or arm a cut that had bled."

"So you are trying to tell us," I came in, "that we should have been looking for someone who had easy access to the house, had no cut on his person and had an alibi for 6.30. In other words, you are saying that young Anderson was the person who killed his parents."

"I am," he said smugly. "If your parents have a lot of money but are not prepared to finance you in the way you think proper, you may decide to kill them to inherit their fortune. But, if you do so, who would then be the prime suspect?"

"You would be."

"Precisely. And, since you know how they illegally acquired their fortune, you devise a plot that seems to point the finger, not at you, but at the people from whom your parents and others stole the money that made all these people very rich."

"So you kill the driver of the bus whom you can most easily trace and then the couple whose address he gave you before he died," Beaumont suggested.

"And, after you have killed your parents," Forsyth added, "you intend to get rid of whichever of the remaining couples you find it easiest to get to. If the killings stopped with your parents, the police might get just a trifle suspicious."

"But he was playing golf at 6.30 and his mother was alive then," said Fletcher doggedly. "The neighbour can attest to that."

"If you have a girl friend who is not overly scrupulous, and is happy to help you to spend the fortune you will, if she helps you, inherit," suggested the Chief. "she can put on a night dress, tie a rope to some object in the living room, put the other end around her wrists and enact the scene laid on for the benefit of the nosy neighbour and then rapidly leave the premises by a back route."

“This is all speculation,” Penny said. “Where is the proof that will convince a jury? Defence Counsel would laugh your notions to scorn.”

“Young Anderson is far too cunning by half,” said Forsyth. “To add verisimilitude to his elaborately staged scene, he added the touch about the cut, putting a spot of someone else’s blood on the glass and scattering Elastoplasts around the sitting room. And, in that action, he told me that he was the killer.”

“How could that tell you that he was the murderer?” asked a bewildered Fletcher.

“A person who had cut his hand in a house that he had presumably never been into before,” explained the great man, “would go to the medicine cabinet, open it and look inside. And what would he see there?”

The light had dawned. I could see where the Chief was going.

“A clearly marked packet of Bandaids.”

“Which any stranger would immediately have opened and used,” stated Forsyth. “Why would he open a tobacco tin to see if it contained Elastoplast?”

“Only someone who stayed in the house,” I declared, “would go to the tin to use up the Elastoplast it contained before thinking of opening a new, untouched packet of Bandaids.”

"Precisely."

"You've convinced me," said Beaumont, "but the Procurator Fiscal may require more than that."

"Which I am happy to provide. I rang up Inspector Davidson yesterday and asked him to find out whether Michael Anderson had a regular girl friend and, if so, to have her at the St Andrews police station when I arrived there in a time of about an hour later. It did not take a great effort to convince her that the game was up and that she was likely to spend the next thirty years in prison as an accessory in a series of cold blooded murders. On the other hand, if she cooperated fully and told us all she knew, she could be tried on a lesser charge and be out in less than ten years. She is a realist. She also has more concern for her own wellbeing than for that of Anderson. She gave us all we wanted and Michael, once he saw that he was well and truly caught, has admitted to everything. All most satisfactory."

"If the money that Ballantine was carrying was mob money to be laundered," enquired Fletcher, "why was no effort made to get it back or to exact vengeance on those who had stolen it?"

"My theory would be," said Forsyth, "that, although I am sure that that course of action would have been advocated, wiser counsels prevailed. The mobs these days attempt to be inconspicuous. If they succeed in that, people tend to ignore them and their activities. It is when they outrage the citizens by doing unlawful things in the full blaze of publicity that people rise up in wrath and the gangs are hounded."

"You mean that, if they had gone around killing those who had stolen the money," said Beaumont, "the subsequent sweep against them would have cost them a lot more money than they lost when Ballantine died."

"Exactly. They had found a good method of getting their ill gotten gains to this country to be laundered and wanted to keep their heads down. So they accepted the losses and did nothing to stir up the authorities against them."

He sent off Fletcher to buy Glenlivets for everyone, Penny agreeing to join us rather than have gin. That lady was sitting gazing at the great man in awe and I could see that she was trying to come up with a plan that would land her in his bed. Like so many new recruits to the squad, she had regarded him as just another copper with an inflated reputation until he had solved by brilliant reasoning a case that had had the rest of us baffled. Now she had fallen under his spell. But, where the others who had preceded her had been content to worship from afar, Penny wanted the great man in bed as her lover. It would be interesting to watch the contest she was about to initiate develop. Penny was a very determined operator but I knew enough about Forsyth to realise that he would resist all her advances. She was not really his type and he was not, as far as I knew, and that was pretty far, into promiscuity. He was also somewhat old fashioned and had strong views as to how someone in his position should deal with female underlings.

I looked across at Beaumont and saw that he had come to the same conclusion as I. He raised his eyebrows at me and shook his head. I nodded and turned my attention back to Penny.

I hoped that things would not get to the stage where I would have to get rid of Penny from the squad. I was convinced that she would make a valuable member of the team and I would be very sorry to lose her, But, if her actions looked as if they would disrupt the team, she would have to go.

But all that was for the future. For the present, I looked forward to a convivial session while we celebrated another triumph for the Chief. And a later session with Millie where, after I had expounded to her the Chief's solution of the case, we could celebrate another Forsyth triumph suitably in my bed.

www.ingramcontent.com/pod-product-compliance
Ingram Content Group UK Ltd.
Pitfield, Milton Keynes, MK11 3LW, UK
UKHW041943190726
13854UKWH00004B/1762